The
Return
of the Railway
Children

Scholastic Children's Books
An imprint of Scholastic Ltd
Euston House, 24 Eversholt Street, London, NW1 1DB, UK
Registered office: Westfield Road, Southam, Warwickshire, CV47 0RA
SCHOLASTIC and associated logos are trademarks and/or
registered trademarks of Scholastic Inc.

First published in the UK by Scholastic Ltd, 2018

Trade ISBN 978 1407 18489 0

Clubs & Fairs ISBN 978 1407 18838 6

A CIP catalogue record for this book
is available from the British Library.

Printed by CPI Group (UK) Ltd, Croydon, CR0 4YY
Papers used by Scholastic Children's Books are made
from wood grown in sustainable forests.

1 3 5 7 9 10 8 6 4 2

www.scholastic.co.uk

The
Return
of the Railway
Children

Lou Kuenzler

SCHOLASTIC

To Hans, who was a "Railway Child" too –
much love, LK

"I wonder if the railway misses us . . .
we never go to see it now."
The Railway Children *by E. Nesbit (1906)*

Contents

Chapter One

Goodbye, Piccadilly

They were not railway children to begin with.

In fact, at first there was just one child. Edith lived alone with her mother in war-torn London while enemy planes dropped bombs on the city every night. Back then, if Edie thought about railways at all, it wasn't roaring steam trains puffing past woods and country fields. It was more likely to be the underground sort, with dark tracks and gloomy tunnels running deep beneath the battered city

1

streets. Edie spent so many long nights huddled in Piccadilly Tube station, amongst hundreds of other Londoners hiding from the air raids, that she began to forget what it was like to sleep in the comfort of her own soft bed.

The Tube station was only a five-minute stroll across Piccadilly Circus from the tiny attic flat on Glasshouse Street where Edie lived with her mother. Yet, every time the siren sounded, there was always a mad last-minute dash to get safely underground.

"Perhaps I ought to go down early next time and save us a good space," said Edie one spring evening as the wailing siren warned them to hurry and take shelter yet again. She'd heard of other people doing this – old ladies or mothers nursing babies, staying in the station all day, holding on to the best sleeping spots right down on the platform, furthest underground, away from the bombs, but with a good wall to lean against while you slept.

"Nonsense, sweetheart," answered Phyllis – or Fliss, as Edie always called her mother. It was all she could manage when she'd try to say "Phyllis" as a little girl. She never called her "Mum" or "Mother" or "Ma". Fliss seemed more like a big sister to Edie than that. "It's a sweet thought, darling, but you'd die of boredom." Fliss kissed the top of Edie's head as she leant over her and reached a silk scarf from the peg behind the door.

Trust Fliss to worry more about being bored than being hit by a bomb, thought Edie. She fidgeted anxiously with the buttons on her coat as Fliss stood in front of the mirror, tucking her long auburn hair under the scarf and putting a fresh dab of scarlet lipstick on her lips.

"But once the siren's sounded, it means German planes have already been spotted over the city. Bombs could start dropping at any moment," Edie said, rushing to the sink and filling a big flask with cold water from the tap so they'd have something to drink. Fliss had promised to make tea earlier so that it would be ready to take with them if the air-raid warning came, but she must have forgotten about it. Edie sighed under her breath and snatched up a pile of blankets she had folded by the door, balancing the flask on top of them.

"Nearly done." Fliss patted her lipstick dry then sprinkled her handkerchief with a little Chanel perfume, the exotic French scent she always wore.

"You don't need perfume now!" groaned Edie. "Come on!"

"I *always* need perfume!" Fliss's blue eyes twinkled. "Especially *now!*" One of Fliss's old friends was a pilot who had recently brought her a big bottle of the perfume from France, even though rationing was supposed to have made it almost impossible to get hold of. Fliss often got little gifts from her friends in the air force; before the war, she had learned to fly planes herself and had even crossed the channel to Paris in a tiny bright yellow biplane called a Tiger Moth. *That's the thing about Fliss,* thought Edie: *she's always on the hunt for adventure.*

But with war raging in the skies above Britain, Edie couldn't help feeling glad her mother's flying days were over. Fliss was helping out in the offices at the Air Ministry instead. "The most excitement I get these days is flying a paper aeroplane!" she moaned on an almost daily basis.

"Ready!" she cried now, putting a last drop of Chanel perfume behind her ear and grabbing Edie's hand. "Let's go."

They dashed out of their peacock-green front door, letting it bang closed behind them.

Edie almost tripped, she ran so fast down the steep stairs from their attic flat. It was horribly busy as they darted across Piccadilly and squeezed into the

Underground station. But Fliss led the way, smiling and greeting everybody as she ducked through the crowd in the ticket hall. By some miracle, they managed to find a spot just big enough for the two of them on the end of the platform against the wall.

"See, you old worrier!" Fliss grinned and put her arm round Edie's shoulder as they snuggled down together. "I told you we'd be all right."

"I know." Edie couldn't help smiling too. Things did have a habit of working out when Fliss was around. Edie gave a sigh of relief; she was glad they'd managed to get such a perfect spot. Without it, they'd have had to sleep on the escalators, where the sound of falling bombs could be heard all through the night. Edie shuddered at the thought. Even though it was hot and stuffy on the platform, at least it felt safe – like an underground cave, deep beneath the city – and you couldn't hear a thing that was going on up above.

The man beside them had turned his back and was already snoring loudly. Edie wished she could sleep like that, but she knew it would be a restless night. She didn't really mind being squashed in amongst strangers, not if Fliss was here with her. She could just about bear the constant noise of rustling, chatter and snoring too – even the heat. But the worst thing about so many bodies being squeezed into the airless tunnels together was the smell. There were only a few makeshift toilets between everyone, and the stench from them filled the air. Some people brought their own chamber pots or tin buckets and used those, squatting on the edge of the platform, but Edie was so embarrassed by the thought, she'd rather have climbed back up to the street to be hit by a bomb. The best thing for it was to cross your legs, hold tight and pray for the all-clear siren.

Meanwhile, she tried not to breathe too deeply and snuggled up against Fliss's shoulder.

"Here!" As if reading her thoughts, Fliss passed her the handkerchief she had sprinkled with Chanel. "Have a whiff of this."

Edie smiled as the rich, musky scent of the perfume filled her nostrils. She'd felt so cross with Fliss earlier, for not hurrying while the siren sounded and forgetting to make tea – the sort of practical things that everybody else's mothers always seemed to do – but now she couldn't think of anything better than having a squirt of exotic French perfume to sniff.

"Trust you to think of it!" she whispered as Fliss stroked her hair.

None of the other girls at school had mothers anything at all like Fliss. Even though she was at least ten years older than most of them, she seemed far more glamorous. They smelt of sickly-sweet lily-of-the-valley scent or plain carbolic soap – not expensive French perfume.

"My mother doesn't approve of French perfume," Edie's form captain, Olive Paterson, had said once. "Nor red lipstick."

"Oh!" Edie had just nodded. But inside she felt as if she'd been punched. She knew that what Olive was really saying was that her mother did not approve of Fliss.

Fliss wasn't married. She never had been. Not even when Edie was born. She had always raised her alone, just the two of them.

And if Edie ever tried to find out anything about her father, all Fliss would ever say was that he had been "no good". "He fled like the wind as soon as I told him I was expecting his baby. If he's foolish enough not to want to be part of our lives, my darling, then we don't need him! We're Fliss and Edie – just fine by ourselves."

And they were fine ... *mostly*. But, as fine and happy as they were, Edie would still have liked to know more about her disappearing father. She wished there was a photograph at least, so she could see his face and imagine him sometimes. Or a name. She didn't even have that. No one knew who he was – except Fliss of course. And maybe Aunt Roberta.

Once, a year or so ago – before the war – when she'd thought Olive Paterson was going to be her best friend at school, Edie had tried to explain. "I don't have a father, you see. Not really," she began.

But Olive had laughed so hard she nearly fell off her chair.

"Of course you've got a father, Edie," Olive sneered. "Everyone has a father, otherwise you wouldn't have been born."

"I know that," blundered Edie. "It's just that mine is. . ." She searched her mind, trying to come up with the right thing to say. "Mine has been mislaid!" Edie beamed, delighted to have thought of such a grown-up way of putting it.

"*Mislaid*?" Olive laughed louder than ever. "You make him sound like a tatty old umbrella that's been left on a train. Why don't you go to the lost property office at Waterloo Station and see if somebody's handed him in there?" Then she ran out into the playground screaming with laughter. For weeks after that, Olive and most of the rest of her form referred to Edie as Edith Umbrella.

Yet, if the girls in her class were bad, their mothers were far worse. They were always looking down their noses at her, and Edie had even overheard two of them whispering about her at the school carol concert last year.

"That's the little girl who was born out of wedlock," said one, pointing at her from behind her hymn book. "She lives alone with her unmarried mother."

"No better than a stray cat on the street," hissed the other.

Edie's eyes had stung with tears, but she wouldn't let herself cry. It would have seemed unfair to Fliss somehow. She always tried her best to be a good mother, even if she was a little disorganized and never sewed Edie's name tapes on and burnt the cakes she'd baked for harvest festival. But there were so many other things she was good at – like flying aeroplanes and telling stories and making Edie laugh.

It didn't matter now, anyway. School was going to close after Easter because there weren't enough girls to keep it going any more. Olive Paterson and her family had left London as soon as war broke out. They'd gone to live in their big manor house somewhere in Wiltshire.

Good riddance! thought Edie. She wouldn't miss Olive or her snooty friends one little bit.

Lots of the other girls had gone away too, the rich ones to their own country houses or to boarding schools, far away from the bombs. A few had joined local evacuees being shipped off to farms and villages. But Fliss had promised she wouldn't send Edie away. They would stay here together and muddle through somehow.

"Close your eyes," Fliss whispered now, waving the scented hankie under Edie's nose. "Smell this and imagine we are not in this horrid old Tube station after all . . . we're in the Café de Paris."

"Oh, I wish we were!" Edie closed her eyes and sniffed deeply. She loved going to the Café de Paris. Fliss knew a pretty young chorus girl there called Lottie, and they often went to watch her dance. The basement jazz club was just about the most glamorous place on earth, with glass lights shaped like flower petals and a sweeping double staircase, which Edie always worried she would fall down, headfirst, tripping over her own feet. They had sheltered there all night during an air raid last week. While Fliss and Lottie danced until dawn, Edie had curled up on a makeshift bed of soft fur coats in the cloakroom. The cafe was so deep underground it was said to be bombproof.

"Go to sleep and pretend you're there now!" whispered Fliss, waving the handkerchief again and swaying gently as Edie dozed against her shoulder, slumped on the hard floor of the Tube station. Fliss began to hum the tune to "Oh, Johnny, Oh", one of the songs which "Snakehips" Johnson, the famous band leader at the cafe, liked to play.

Edie closed her eyes, listening as Fliss sang softly in her ear, and breathing in the rich musky scent of Chanel. As she drifted off to sleep, she imagined she really was in the cafe, amongst all the beautiful dancers, like Cinderella at a royal ball.

Hours later, Edie woke with a start. She reached out, expecting to touch soft furs beneath her, but felt only the cold damp floor of the Underground station. Then she remembered where she was. She wasn't in the Café de Paris at all. She was down in the Tube, squashed up on the platform like a sardine in a can.

"Come on!" whispered Fliss. "The all clear's sounded. We can go home."

It was morning as they stumbled back up the steps and out into the bright spring light and bustle of Piccadilly Circus. Signs of the war were all around: even the famous statue of Eros had been covered up with sandbags to keep the winged god safe from bombs.

Edie blinked and rubbed her eyes. She always hated this moment, coming back above ground. What if their flat had been bombed in the night, and there was nothing left but sky and fallen rubble where her pretty blue bedroom had once been? She forced herself to look towards Glasshouse Street and breathed a sigh of relief. She could see the tip of the turret on their high attic roof, pointing proudly to the sky like a lighthouse.

"All clear!" she murmured. But as soon as she glanced in the opposite direction she saw ambulances and fire engines streaming out of Coventry Street and down Haymarket to their right.

"Somewhere close has been hit," said a woman as she squeezed past them with a cat in a basket. "I'm just glad my Ginger was safe."

As they drew closer, Edie could see a barricade

half-drawn across the road. People in suits and overalls were hurrying to work and, in amongst the hustle and bustle of the regular morning routine, wardens were shouting and waving their arms.

"Direct hit last night! Hell of a mess," sighed an ARP warden, as two firemen with blackened faces sat on the edge of the pavement nestling big tin mugs of tea.

"Oh no!" whispered Edie. She bit her lip. Somehow she knew, even before they saw the shattered building, that it was the Café de Paris.

"It can't be true," gasped Fliss, steadying herself against Edie's shoulder.

There was nothing left but the balcony, suspended like an arch in the sky. Three whisky glasses were still resting on a little table, which seemed to hang in mid-air as if waiting for the drinkers to return. In the crater below, the grand piano sat unharmed in the rubble, covered in shards of twinkling glass from the splintered flower-petal lights.

"So much for being bombproof, eh?" shrugged the warden as they stood and stared. There was a horrible, thick, burnt smell of smoke and gas.

"Did everyone get out?" asked Edie desperately. "Did they all get away?"

The warden shook his head solemnly. "Not all, I'm afraid, miss. It took a direct hit. Right through the roof."

Edie shuddered. Then she saw Lottie, the chorus-line dancer they knew. She was standing on the opposite side of the street, shivering in her tiny dance costume, which was more like a ballet tutu than a real dress. The huge white ostrich feather in her hair was grey with dust. Fliss grabbed a blanket from an ambulance man and dashed across the road to wrap it around Lottie's shoulders.

"It's all right, poppet," she whispered. "It's all over now."

Edie followed. She stretched out her hand and rubbed Lottie's back, just like Fliss did whenever she was sad. Tears streamed down the dancer's pale, delicate face, clearing channels like little rivers through the dust and soot. "Me and the girls just missed it," she sobbed. "We were waiting in the wings, about to come on. Another minute or so and we'd have been on stage. . . But Snakehips was right there. Right underneath it. He was just starting the opening bars of 'Oh, Johnny, Oh!'" She gulped for breath. "And poor Mr Poulson, the manager, too."

Edie felt sick. She wanted to turn and run away

but she couldn't move. She stood rooted to the spot as Lottie shook her head and wiped away the tears with the back of her hand.

"God rest their souls," Lottie whispered, and she staggered away up the street.

"Poor lass," said the warden. "Anyone who got out was lucky to survive."

"Buckingham Palace was hit too," said a fireman who was searching through the rubble. "But the Royal Family are safe."

"God save the King!" roared a soldier with a bandage over one eye. Edie wasn't sure if he'd come from the cafe or just been walking down the street, but he was swigging from a dusty bottle of champagne that he must have found in the rubble. He offered Fliss a sip but she shook her head.

"Let's go home, sweetie." She grabbed Edie's hand. "There's nothing we can do here. It's just too beastly."

As Fliss pulled her away, Edie spotted a high-heeled silver shoe lying in the gutter. Just one, as if it had been dropped by Cinderella at the ball . . . except that it was covered in dust and soot.

She shivered.

"That's it! I'm getting you out of this city," said

Fliss, almost dragging Edie back past the boarded-up statue of Eros.

"You mean we're leaving?" said Edie. "When?" But Fliss didn't even seem to hear her.

"I should have done it months ago," she said, talking more to herself than to Edie. "What kind of mother am I?"

"Where will we go?" said Edie, tugging at her sleeve. "London's our home."

"Not any more," said Fliss. She put her arm round Edie's shoulder but her voice was still shaking as she spoke. "Seeing the cafe like that has brought me to my senses. Suppose we'd been there again last night. You could have been killed ... and now school's closing too." She stopped in the middle of the street. "I've made up my mind," she said. "You'll have to go to Aunt Roberta in the country."

"Aunt Roberta? In Yorkshire?" Edie gasped. "What about you?" she asked, panic rising in her throat. "Will you come too?" She had never been anywhere without Fliss before.

"No." Fliss shook her head. "I'm afraid not, poppet."

"But I've never met Aunt Roberta," said Edie. "You told me you fell out with her when I was still a baby."

"Oh, don't worry about any of that!" Fliss brushed away her protests and began hurrying down the street again. "You're family and there's a war on. None of that nonsense matters now."

Edie ran to catch up. "Then why did you and Aunt Roberta stop speaking to each other in the first place?" she blurted out.

"Oh, it was nothing, really. I suppose she disapproved of the way I lived my life," said Fliss vaguely. She waved her hands in the air as if dismissing any further questions.

Edie felt a sickening guilt creeping up into her chest. She was certain she knew exactly why Aunt Roberta disapproved of Fliss. It would be the same thing it always was with grown-ups. Her – Edie. The illegitimate, unwanted baby girl, born when Fliss wasn't married.

"Don't look so worried. Uncle Peter will be there too," said Fliss. "You'll love Pete. We used to go with him to the seaside sometimes. Do you remember?"

Edie shook her head. She had only been about two or three years old at the time. But at least he didn't seem to disapprove of her. He sent a postal order on her birthday every year.

"I'm sorry, sweetie." Fliss laid her hand on Edie's

arm. "I wish I could come with you. But there's something I have to do. Something important."

"What is it?" asked Edie slowly. She knew she wasn't going to like the answer.

"I'm going to fly planes again," said Fliss.

"Fly?" Edie stared at her mother. "You're going to fly planes for the war?" She felt as if her knees might give way beneath her. "But it's so dangerous."

Fliss squeezed her arm. "I have to, darling. They're asking women to help out now." Edie could hear the excitement in her mother's voice. She felt a stab of jealousy. Fliss loved flying more than anything. Perhaps even more than looking after her, she thought angrily.

Edie stopped dead in her tracks. "You knew all along!" she said, suddenly realizing that this wasn't something Fliss had thought of on the spur of the moment at all. It had nothing to do with those poor people at the Café de Paris, or school closing, or any of the rest of it. That was all just an excuse. Fliss must have been planning it for weeks.

"They want any of us who can fly to join the Air Transport Auxiliary," said Fliss quietly, but her cheeks were flushed. "The chaps in the RAF need planes delivered to them from all over the country.

I'll be bringing aircraft from factories and airfields and flying them to wherever they're needed." She tried to take Edie's hand, but Edie shrugged her off. "It's all part of the war effort, poppet. It's the right thing to do."

Edie sighed, blinking back tears. It was pointless to argue with Fliss when she'd decided something.

"Stupid, rotten war!" she muttered under her breath. In spite of all Fliss's promises that they would stay together, she was being shunted off to the country to live with a strange aunt she didn't know. Meanwhile, Fliss was going to risk her life flying planes and Edie knew there was nothing she could do to stop her.

Chapter Two

Smoke, Steam and Suitcases

The hustle and bustle of King's Cross seemed to Edie more like an army base than a train station. Soldiers in khaki uniform were hurrying to and from trains or sitting on their kit bags smoking cigarettes and laughing.

The last few days had been a constant flurry of activity, with both Edie and Fliss packing and preparing to go away. Fliss was already wearing her smart navy-blue Air Transport Auxiliary uniform with gold ATA wings on her chest. She looked beautiful and men turned to stare as they squeezed through the crowds. One young soldier even whistled as they passed. Edie wished they'd all stop gawping. She wanted Fliss to herself – just for these last few minutes before the train.

When they eventually reached the platform, the train was already billowing smoke; clouds of it were swirling up to the station roof like fog.

"It's as if the train's a mighty dragon!" Edie shouted above the noise.

Fliss laughed and her face broke into a wide smile. "That's what we used to call them when I was your age." She crouched down and straightened the gas mask hanging in its little cardboard box around Edie's neck. "When we lived at Three Chimneys, Aunt Roberta, Uncle Peter and I used to wave to the 9.15 train and ask it to send our love to Father as it roared past on its way to London. We called it the Green Dragon."

Edie felt a sudden wriggle of excitement in her tummy. Although she was going to miss Fliss dreadfully, she couldn't believe she was really going to see Three Chimneys for herself. She had grown up hearing so many tales about her mother's time at the house beside the railway and the adventures the three children had all those years ago, back before the Great War.

"I'll do the same," said Edie excitedly. "When I get to Three Chimneys, I'll wave to the Green Dragon and ask it to send my love to you."

Fliss smiled. "I won't actually be in London, of course." She glanced anxiously over her shoulder at the poster on the wall. CARELESS TALK COSTS LIVES, it warned. She leant closer and whispered in Edie's ear as if a German spy might be sitting on a bench right behind them. "I'll be living on the airbase from now on. On the south coast."

"I know. Then you'll be flying planes up and down the country," Edie whispered back, although she didn't want to think about it. "The smoke from the train will float up into the sky like a cloud. It'll find you and bring you my love, wherever you are."

"Oh, sweetie, that's a wonderful idea!" Fliss threw her arms around Edie and kissed her cheek.

"Excuse me. Mind your backs," said an official-looking lady in a green hat, although there was plenty of room to get by anyway. She strode off along the platform like the Pied Piper, leading a straggly line of evacuees with luggage labels tied around their necks. Edie felt a surge of pride that she'd be travelling alone with no one to look after her. But the feeling vanished as a tall blond-haired boy raised his eyebrows as he passed her on the end of the line. Edie blushed, guessing at once that she'd have a bright red lipstick mark from Fliss's kiss in the middle of her cheek. She spat on her fingers and rubbed her face.

"Come on! Keep up, will you!" The blond boy turned and shouted over his shoulder. For a moment Edie thought he was hollering at her. Then she saw a tiny girl struggling towards them. She couldn't have been more than about five years old – her suitcase was almost as big as she was.

"Brute! Why doesn't he help her?" frowned Edie. It was obvious they were brother and sister. The girl had the same bright blonde hair, except hers fell in tight curls around her hot, red face. She was stumbling along with the suitcase banging against her knees. In her other hand, she was clutching a little woollen elephant. She had to stop every three or four paces to swap sides.

Edie couldn't stand it. "Here! Let me help you."

She scooped up the suitcase before the little girl could say a word. Fliss leapt forward too and picked up her coat, which was dragging behind her. The girl beamed up at them with delight. As she smiled she showed two big gaps where she must have recently lost some wobbly teeth.

"Thank you!" she grinned. "I could manage myself. Honest I could. It's only that Mr Churchill wanted to hold my hand and he did make such a fuss." She waved the tubby knitted elephant in the air. Clearly he was the Mr Churchill she was talking about. Edie wondered if the *other* Mr Churchill, the busy important prime minister, would mind sharing his famous name with a cuddly toy.

"I expect Mr Churchill is very heavy to carry." Edie laughed.

"Of course he is," said the girl, her face deadly serious. "He's an elephant." Without waiting to be asked, she slipped her hand into Edie's and skipped down the platform beside her. Edie didn't even mind that the little girl had squeezed in between her and Fliss in their last moments together. She had always wanted a little brother or sister of her own, and for a moment she secretly imagined they might all be one family, setting off for a holiday together at the seaside, perhaps. But when the older boy turned round again he scowled furiously.

"Don't make a nuisance of yourself, Greta," he huffed. "You can carry your own case perfectly well."

"It's no bother!" said Edie and Fliss at exactly the same time. They grinned at each other.

But the boy walked back and snatched the suitcase from Edie's hand. "We can manage, thank you," he said stiffly, and he bustled Greta away, following the Pied-Piper woman down the platform.

"Why don't you join them?" suggested Fliss. "It might be nice to have some other children in your carriage."

Edie shook her head. She wouldn't have minded chattering to little Greta, but her big brother looked so grumpy and stuck-up and all the other evacuees seemed to know each other.

"I'll be fine here, honestly," she said, spotting an empty compartment and opening the carriage door. "I've got my book."

She knew she was going to have to be very grown-up from now on. She was going to have to manage by herself.

"All right, then," said Fliss encouragingly. "Spread

your things out a bit and you might even have it to yourself. The troops can get a bit rowdy."

"I'll be fine," said Edie again, though she wished her voice wouldn't crack like that. "If there's any trouble at all, I'll go and find the Pied Piper."

"Who?" said Fliss.

Edie put her nose in the air and imitated the snooty woman in charge of the evacuees.

"Ah!" Fliss laughed and wagged her finger. "Just one thing. Do make sure you look after your ration book," she said seriously. "It's in the pocket of your suitcase, with your socks. Give it to Aunt Roberta when you arrive or she won't be able to feed you so much as a slice of bread and dripping until the end of the war!"

"I will," said Edie. "But, Fliss. . .?" They had closed the door between them now and Edie was leaning out of the window while Fliss stood on the platform. "She does know I'm coming, doesn't she? Aunt Roberta, I mean?"

Edie was worried Fliss still hadn't spoken to her, not even to make arrangements.

"Of course, sweetheart. It's all tickety-boo." Fliss smiled brightly. "I sent a telegram. Roberta's going to meet you at the station when the train gets in.

I'd deliver you myself, only I'm due at the base first thing in the morning and. . ."

"It's all right." Edie tried to smile too, but she was suddenly overcome with a wave of nerves. It wasn't the journey she was worried about. It was the thought of going all the way to Yorkshire to stay with a disapproving aunt who didn't even want her there. She'd rather stay here in London and face the bombs. Most of all, she wanted to stay with Fliss.

"Please," she said. "Can't we just—"

But there was a great hiss of steam, a puff of smoke and a clank of pistons. The guard on the platform shouted something that sounded like, "All aboard!" Doors slammed, a whistle blew and the huge engine began to move.

"Goodbye!" cried Edie, her heart thumping.

"*Bon voyage*, sweetheart!" Fliss waved her handkerchief. Even with her nostrils full of smoke and soot, Edie caught a whiff of Chanel perfume. "Have fun!" Fliss ran along the platform as the engine gathered speed.

"And you be careful!" said Edie. "Please!" But her words were drowned out. Fliss was lost in the smoke as the train thundered away.

Edie wished she had asked Fliss for her handkerchief. It wasn't that she was crying. "Of course not," she told herself, wiping her cheeks with her sleeve. It was just that there was soot and smoke in her eyes.

Even so, she was glad to have the compartment to herself so that nobody could hear her sniff. She listened as hoards of rowdy troops thundered up and down the corridor outside. Some of them were singing, and their loud voices frightened Edie a little. She wished more than ever that Fliss was with her. But she took a deep breath and did as she'd suggested, spreading her coat out across the seats. "I've always wanted an adventure of my own, and now I've got one," she whispered, trying to be firm with herself. Underneath all the worry, she felt excitement squirming in her tummy too.

She opened her book and tried to read, but she couldn't take in a word, not with all the bustle and noise on the train and the bombed-out buildings of London slipping by outside the window.

The sliding door opened suddenly and a man with a band of red tartan around his regimental beret almost fell through it.

"Sorry, lassie. I'll leave you in peace," he said,

crashing backwards against the door frame as the train rattled on.

"No, honestly, it's fine," Edie called after him guiltily, but he had already stumbled away, leaving the compartment door wide open.

She got to her feet and poked her head out into the corridor. She was shocked to see gaggles of men standing in the aisle or sitting on their kit bags.

"Oh, dear," muttered Edie. They were off to fight for King and Country, or heading home for a well-earned leave. The least they deserved was a proper seat. She screwed up her courage, stuffed her coat on to the luggage rack and cleared her throat.

"Hello." Nobody seemed to hear her. She coughed and tried again more loudly. "Excuse me. There are seats in here if anyone wants them."

"Good!" said a clear sharp voice from further down the corridor. But it wasn't one of the soldiers who had spoken. It was the Pied Piper. She appeared in the doorway to the next carriage, a long pheasant feather bobbing in the top of her green hat.

"If you've got space, little girl, we'll take it," she said, almost pushing Edie aside as she poked her beaky nose into the compartment to inspect it. "Perfect. We're two seats short in our carriage." She glanced at the list on her clipboard and then peered over her shoulder. "Where is that wretched child? I told him to follow me." She sighed deeply. "I thought *his* sort were supposed to be organized..."

Edie had no idea what that meant, but a moment later, the grumpy-looking blond boy from the station appeared, lugging his suitcase down the corridor. Greta skipped after him, swinging Mr Churchill by his long grey trunk. A soldier was carrying her suitcase for her. She gave him her best toothy grin as he heaved it into the luggage rack by the window.

"There you go, General," he said, saluting her smartly and going on his way.

Greta giggled with delight. "I'm not a general. I'm a girl!" she called after him.

"Settle down, now!" snapped the Pied Piper, as Greta flopped backwards on to a seat and grinned at Edie.

The boy sat down too, sighing heavily and barely even glancing at Edie as he stared out of the window. Edie guessed he must be only a year or so older than she was, but he looked so stern and serious it was hard to tell.

"Righty-ho!" The Pied Piper scribbled something on her clipboard. "You've got your sandwiches and a flask of tea. I'm just in the other carriage if there's any trouble." She wagged her finger at the three children. "I don't want to hear a peep out of any of you." She appeared to have forgotten that she wasn't in charge of Edie at all.

She stepped out of the compartment and closed the door behind her. Even the soldiers in the corridor seemed to settle down under her strict stare. But, the minute she marched away out of sight, Greta bounced off her seat and flopped on to the one next to Edie.

"Hello," she said with an enormous grin. "I'm Greta. I met you before. And this is Mr Churchill, remember?" She held up the grey knitted elephant.

Edie smiled. "Of course I remember. Hello. I'm Edie." She shook the elephant's trunk and the little girl's hand, then glanced towards the boy.

He made no effort to introduce himself but began to flick through the pages of a large book about aeroplanes.

How rude, thought Edie. From the furious look on his face you'd think it was she who had interrupted his peace and quiet, not the other way round.

But Greta seemed determined they should all be friends. She leapt to her feet again.

"This is Gus, my big brother," she said. "His real name is—"

"Gus will do just fine," the boy snapped. "Honestly, Greta. We're only sharing a carriage for an hour or two. There's no need to tell perfect strangers our entire life story."

"And there's no need for you to be so rude!" said Edie. The words were out of her mouth before she could stop herself.

"'Zactly!" Greta folded her arms and nodded in agreement.

"We're just trying to be friendly. That's all," muttered Edie.

Gus sighed and continued to stare at the pictures of aeroplanes.

"My mother's going to fly planes, you know," said Edie, trying a different tack. Perhaps he wouldn't be so stuck-up if he realized how important Fliss's new job was going to be.

"Yes. I saw her," he said. "At the station. She was the woman wearing the Air Transport Auxiliary uniform, I suppose?"

"That's right." Edie felt a swell of pride.

"Hmm!" He flicked over another page in his book. "The ATA aren't part of the proper air force, you know. They only deliver planes to the real pilots. It's like driving a bus or something. That's why they've let women join. They don't go into battle or anything."

"But..." Edie opened and closed her mouth in fury. "The pilots in the ATA risk their lives every day," she said, remembering how Fliss had come into the flat a few months ago, tears streaming down her face as she handed Edie a copy of the evening paper. The famous aviator Amy Johnson had been killed trying to land an ATA plane in freezing fog – and she was probably the most experienced female pilot in the world.

Gus lifted his head and looked at Edie properly at last. "Our father is a real fighter pilot," he said. "He's shooting down enemy planes every day."

"Oh!" Edie slumped back in her chair. She knew she'd been trying to show off about Fliss, but now she felt so deflated it was almost as if she had been shot down herself.

She stared out of the window, unable to think of anything else to say. London was far behind them and the train was now steaming along between green fields. It was going to be a long, awkward journey all the way to Yorkshire.

Chapter Three

The Great Leap

While Gus stared sulkily at his book of aeroplanes, Greta chattered like a little monkey, bouncing up and down on her seat. Edie soon learnt that the two children had been raised in London by their father. Their mother had died when Greta was born.

"Then Papa was taken away by soldiers and we had to go and live with Grandma Perkins," Greta explained, her big blue eyes brimming with tears. Edie squeezed her hand.

"They weren't soldiers, they were airmen," Gus snapped. "And they didn't take him away, silly. I've told you a hundred times: they were men from Papa's squadron in the RAF. They were all heading back to the base together."

Greta shrugged and wiped her nose on Mr Churchill's ears. "Grandma Perkins' flat smells funny," she said. "But a bomb fell down the chimbley when we were in the air-raid shelter. It 'sploded and all Granny Perkins' best plates were busted. I was jolly glad I had Mr Churchill safe with me in the shelter."

Gus raised his eyebrows. "It was more than just plates. The whole building was rubble." Edie saw him swallow hard.

"At least no one was hurt," she said, wishing there was something more she could say. No matter how many times she heard stories like this from the war, it never seemed to get any easier. "It must be . . . well, it must be horrible for your grandma to lose her home like that."

"She's gone to live with Uncle Alan," said Greta, bouncing up and down on the seat again. "In Ease Grimpstid."

"East Grinstead," corrected Gus. "Not that it's anybody's business."

"Wasn't there room for you to go and live there too?" asked Edie, glancing at Gus.

"No!" He sighed. "There wasn't."

"Uncle Alan doesn't like children." Greta sat down with a thump. "Nor does Granny very much," she added, chewing her lip. "Uncle Alan has five pick-your-knees dogs. Granny says they're a lot less bother than we are."

"Pekinese," snapped Gus. "And you're talking nonsense."

"No I'm not!" Greta stuck her chin out. "Granny told the lady postman it would do us good to be 'vacuated to the country and good riddance."

Gus rolled his eyes but Edie could see a blush creeping up his neck.

"Perhaps you'll be evacuated to a farm," she said, trying to change the subject. "With sheep or cows."

"Or piglets?" said Greta with a yawn. "Me and Mr Churchill would like our very own piglet to look after." Her eyelids were starting to droop, and before long she had dozed off, cuddling her elephant, with her head resting on Edie's shoulder.

Gus laid down the aeroplane book, dug in his bag and pulled out his and Greta's ration books, which he began to peer at instead. Edie couldn't imagine there was anything very interesting to see, but whatever it was seemed to make him scowl even more fiercely than before. Eventually he sighed and tossed the little brown booklets carelessly on the seat beside him.

"Anything wrong?" asked Edie.

"No!" Gus shook his head, and the two older children sank back into awkward silence until Greta woke up from her nap at lunchtime.

"Hello, Sleepyhead." Edie smiled as she unpacked the food parcel Fliss had wrapped for her in the pages of one of her old magazines. A carrot sandwich lay on top of a picture of a beautiful young woman powdering her nose. Instead of grating the carrot, Fliss had cut it up with a knife and the chunks were so big they were hard to chew. Fliss was never a brilliant cook, even before wartime rationing made things so difficult. But she had managed to find a bar of Fry's chocolate and put a big red lipstick kiss on the wrapper. Edie smiled.

Gus and Greta had fish-paste sandwiches, which made the whole compartment stink. Greta held her nose and giggled. They gulped them down with swigs from a flask of tea.

Edie couldn't help staring longingly at the flask as she tried hard to swallow a lump of dry carrot.

37

"Do you want some?" asked Greta, following her gaze. "We can share my cup."

"Oh, yes please. If you're sure you don't mind?" said Edie.

"Of course not. I'll give us a top-up," said Greta proudly. She leant forward to grab the flask, which was balanced on the seat beside Gus.

"Careful! That's hot," he warned, snatching for it at the same time. But it was too late. Tea spilled everywhere. It went all over the pages of his aeroplane book and their two ration books, which were lying next to it.

"Now look what you've done!" Gus cried and Greta burst into floods of tears.

"It was an accident," said Edie. If anything, Gus was the one to blame. He should have put the lid back on the flask. And he certainly shouldn't have left their precious documents lying around like that. It was asking for trouble.

Gus ignored her. He grabbed the ration books and began rubbing them hard with the edge of his sweater.

"Don't do that," cried Edie. "You'll make it worse." He was rubbing so hard, the ink where their names were written had smudged and he had almost ripped right through the paper. Edie remembered how strict and serious Fliss had been when giving her instructions to keep her own ration book safe. That showed how important it was. Fliss was never strict or serious about anything.

"You'll need to give your ration books to the people wherever you're billeted," she said. "It's got all your details and everything. They'll need to know your full names."

"Then I can tell them our full names," said Gus, furiously rubbing at the inside pages now.

"And we've got labels," sniffed Greta. "In case we get lost. See?" She held up the luggage tag around her neck.

But Gus's hand shot out and ripped her label from its string. He grabbed his own label too and hurled them both out of the window of the train. "There! Good riddance!"

Edie watched in horror as they fluttered away, out of sight in an instant.

"You shouldn't have done that," she gasped. Was he mad? The Pied Piper would be furious. "Evacuees are supposed to keep their labels on at all times . . ."

"Well, we didn't. We're not parcels. We're people.

We can speak English and explain ourselves. So there!" said Gus. But his hands were shaking. "What's it to you anyway?" he muttered. He had turned bright red and was staring at his feet. "You're not our mother."

"No," said Edie quietly. "I suppose I'm not." She sank back into her seat. Gus was right. It was none of her business. But she couldn't help wondering why he was so keen to tell people his own name rather than letting them read it off their official documents? What difference did it make? Edie glanced over and saw that he was chewing his fingernails. He seemed to be so furious all the time. Perhaps it was just like he said: he didn't want to be sent away and treated like a package. Or maybe he was just worried sick knowing his father was flying planes. The RAF were right in the thick of the action. She crossed her fingers and made a silent wish that Gus and Greta's father would stay safe. Fliss too, of course. The only sound in the carriage was Greta sniffing loudly as she wiped the pages of Gus's precious aeroplane book with Mr Churchill's trunk.

"Leave it," said Gus more gently. Then he laughed. "Wherever we end up, that poor elephant is going to need a good wash!"

"Never!" protested Greta. "Mr Churchill does not like water."

Edie giggled. And, for the briefest moment, all three of them smiled.

"Here," she said, unwrapping the foil from her cherished bar of Fry's. "Who'd like a square of chocolate?"

It was a peace offering she knew even grumpy Gus would not be able to refuse.

Half an hour later, the guard came to check their tickets.

"You're the next stop, Miss," he told Edie as the train chugged between high green hills. "There won't be any signs telling you which station you're at because they've all been taken down in case the Germans invade. This way they won't know where they are, see?"

"Gosh," said Edie. "That's clever."

"We think of everything on the railways, Miss." The guard chuckled as he checked Gus and Greta's tickets too. "You two need to stay on until Maidbridge. That's the next big town, the stop after this young lady here."

"Thank you," said Edie as he helped her take her

suitcase down from the luggage rack and hurried on to the next compartment.

As she began to button her coat, her tummy was suddenly full of butterflies again. In just a few moments she would meet Aunt Roberta for the very first time. The only picture she'd ever seen of her was taken years ago when Aunt Roberta was still a child. It was cut from a newspaper, and Fliss had framed it and hung above the mantelpiece in Glasshouse Street. There was a little caption underneath which read: RAILWAY CHILDREN, and the photograph showed young Fliss, Aunt Roberta and Uncle Peter grinning and wearing their grandest old-fashioned clothes as they stood on a station platform to receive a prize. The very same little station she was about to arrive at, Edie realized. Fliss often told the story of how the three children had saved a train from crashing into a landslide on the line. Bobbie, as Aunt Roberta was always called back then, had the wonderful idea of ripping up the girls' red flannel petticoats and waving them so the driver would know there was danger ahead and stop in time. *That* Bobbie sounded adventurous and fun. You only needed to look at the pictures, and see the way the sisters smiled at each other, to know how well they must have got on as children. But the photograph was taken years ago – long before Aunt Roberta's mysterious falling out with Fliss. Edie couldn't help imagining the grown-up, disapproving Aunt Roberta very differently. She pictured a terrible, angry sort of aunt: the sort who would sigh loudly and glare at her over the top of half-moon spectacles.

The train was slowing now, juddering and hissing steam as they pulled into the station.

"Goodbye. It's been lovely to meet you." Edie held out her hand, which Gus shook stiffly.

"Goodbye and ... er ... thank you for keeping Greta happy." He nodded.

"I've enjoyed it," said Edie, crouching down beside the little girl. "I do hope you end up at a pretty farm. With your very own piglet."

Greta kicked her feet against the seat.

"I don't want you to go," she said. "I want you to be 'vacuated with us."

"I know. I wish that too," said Edie. And it was true. "But I can't. I have to stay here with my aunt." The train was rattling into the station already. She kissed the top of Greta's blonde head and shook Mr Churchill by a dangling leg. "Maybe we can meet in Maidbridge soon."

Greta kicked the seat again.

"Stop making a fuss, Greta," said Gus. "Remember how you promised Papa you'd be brave?"

Greta sniffed. "I am brave," she said. "It's just Mr Churchill who doesn't like it."

"Then you better tell him what an adventure it is going to be," said Edie with a wink.

The train had stopped now and she picked up her suitcase before Greta could burst into tears.

"Toodle-oo, old things. Pip pip!" She giggled, saluting them both and trying her best to sound like a jolly major general. Greta burst into peals of laughter. Edie seized the moment. "Cheerio!" She jumped down from the carriage and shut the door. In all the commotion of parting from the little girl, she had almost forgotten her own nerves about arriving. But her tummy squirmed as she squinted along the platform.

A young red-faced farmer was hauling a crate of chickens out of the guard's van. Their squawks were loud enough to be heard over the hiss of the train.

"Shut up, you daft beggars!" he roared, kicking the crate across the platform with his boot. He looked nothing like the pictures of jolly farmers in the storybooks Edie had read when she was little.

"Good shot, Donny." A skinny porter sauntered down the platform, laughing as the poor chickens screeched. The two men looked so alike, Edie was sure they must be brothers. They were both tall and bony, with the same short-cropped hair and narrow, pointy faces. As the porter reached Edie, he stopped and folded his arms. "You from London?"

She nodded.

"Well, I hope you're not expecting me to carry that?" he said, staring down at her suitcase.

"Oh, no. Of course not," said Edie, stumbling to pick it up. "I can manage."

"Grand!" The porter's lip curled. "Only I don't touch luggage from evacuees." He turned back to the farmer. "You know why that is, don't you, Donny?"

"Aye, Len," he snorted. "On account of the lice!"

"Lice?" Edie was horrified. "I don't have lice," she cried.

The two young men were falling about with laughter. She realized they were teasing her.

"'Course you do," said the porter. "All kids from London have lice."

"Well, I don't!" Edie felt a furious blush creeping up her cheeks. She glanced desperately along the platform. There was no sign of anyone who could be Aunt Roberta. She wanted to jump back on the train with Gus and Greta. Perhaps Aunt Roberta had forgotten about her. Or perhaps she had decided not to come and collect her at all. Suddenly, the dread of being abandoned, alone on the little country train station, so far from home, was much worse than the fear of meeting her formidable aunt at long last. But, just as she felt the panic rising in her throat, she saw the tall figure of a woman in a long cape striding towards her.

She knew at once it was her aunt, even before the porter touched his cap and scurried away. "Afternoon, Nurse Roberta, ma'am." He seemed a little afraid of her as he darted off to help the farmer unload two more large wooden crates from the guard's van.

"Edie!" Aunt Roberta smiled. She was only a few years older than Fliss, but she looked as if she was from another generation – a proper grown-up, like Edie's headmistress at school. As she stepped closer, Edie could see there were lines around her eyes, and the strands of hair poking out from under her headscarf were peppered with grey.

"Hello." Edie shifted uncomfortably, wondering if she ought to hug her. She decided not. Out of the corner of her eye, she caught sight of Greta peering at them through the window of the carriage.

"Thank goodness you're here," said Aunt Roberta. "It was madness of your mother to keep you in London. It is no place for a child in the Blitz." Aunt Roberta sighed as if this was Edie's fault somehow. Edie could imagine her telling Fliss off in the same way. No wonder they'd stopped talking. Fliss hated being told what to do by anybody.

"You're the absolute spit of her, by the way," said Aunt Roberta more gently, as she looked Edie up and down.

"Me? Of Fliss?" Edie gasped. She couldn't tell whether Aunt Roberta thought that was a good thing or not. It was nonsense, anyway. She didn't look anything like the beautiful auburn-haired Fliss, with her perfect straight nose and flashing green eyes. Whenever Edie squinted at herself in the mirror, her own eyes seemed small and dull. Her nose was turned up and her hair was dark – like chocolate, as Fliss always said. Like mud, Edie thought.

"I'd have recognized you anywhere!" said Aunt Roberta. "You could be Phyllis, that first summer we came here. We were always down at the station, bothering poor old Albert Perks."

"Perks, the porter?" cried Edie, as the train hissed behind them. She was delighted to recognize the name from Fliss's stories. "The one who used to be here when you were children?"

"Yes. Long before young Len Snigson, there." Aunt Roberta motioned over her shoulder as the porter slammed a door shut at the far end of the train. "Perks could have shown him a thing or two," she said, shouting over the noise of the building steam. Then, all of a sudden, her face lit up. "Oh, dear!" She laughed and put her hand over her mouth. "We did give that poor man the most dreadful time."

Edie smiled. She felt her tummy relax a little. Perhaps her aunt wasn't going to be as strict and terrible as she'd feared.

The train whistled loudly, making her jump. It was ready to leave. The guard held up a green flag, and Len Snigson hollered down the platform: "Mind yer backs!"

Edie turned to wave goodbye to Gus and Greta, one last time. But, before she could raise a hand, she heard a commotion in the carriage. The door swung wide open and a small figure leapt from the train. In the next instant, Greta had scrambled to Edie's side and flung her arms around her waist.

"I want to go with you!" she wailed. "I don't want to go to the farm. Gussy says there might be rats!"

"Rats? Oh, for goodness' sake!" Now Aunt Roberta sounded just as fierce as Edie had thought she'd be. "You have to get back on the train, little girl. Hurry! It's leaving."

"What's going on?" The Pied Piper poked her head out of a carriage further down the train. "You there," she cried, shaking her clipboard at Greta. "Get back on board, this instant! I'm supposed to take you to the central sorting post at Maidbridge."

The guard appeared at the window too as Len Snigson thundered down the platform towards them. "Get on the train, you little urchin!" He pulled at Greta's shoulders, but she clung like a limpet to Edie's waist.

"Steady on!" snapped Aunt Roberta.

"Stop!" cried Edie, pulling Greta closer. "You're hurting her."

"It's too late, anyway," said Aunt Roberta. And she was right. Smoke shot out of the funnel as the train began to chug away, leaving Greta standing on the station, still clinging to Edie for dear life.

"Now you've blown it! The driver won't stop for nowt," sneered Len Snigson.

Greta looked up at her brother's shocked face as he peered out of the window disappearing down the tracks.

"Gussy," she sobbed, holding out her hand helplessly towards the moving train. And then, screaming twice as loudly, "Mr Churchill! Wait!"

Edie couldn't stand it.

"Please," she cried, running alongside the train and shouting to the Pied Piper and the guard. "Stop the train! Poor Greta can't be left on her own! We'll take her... and Gus too."

"Gracious," the Pied Piper gasped. The train was gathering speed. Before the guard could say a word, the door to Gus's carriage was flung open again. Two suitcases, the woolly elephant and the book about aeroplanes flew on to the platform. The boy himself followed a moment later. There was a dull thud as he landed on the soft verge at the edge of the track, just beyond the station.

Edie gasped loudly, her heart pounding as Gus lay still. *He's dead*, she thought.

But a second later Gus staggered to his feet, unhurt.

The Pied Piper craned her neck to look back down the line.

"There'll be paperwork!" she hollered, waving her clipboard through the steam.

"Indeed!" Aunt Roberta didn't shout, but her voice was loud and crisp and clear. "I suppose there will be."

The train thundered away, taking the Pied Piper with it.

"Now you've done it!" said Len Snigson.

Gus pelted down the platform and scooped Greta up in his arms.

"Don't you ever do anything like that again," he cried, shouting and hugging her all at the same time. Edie ran to them too and, without thinking, threw her arms around them both.

The hug only lasted a moment before Gus and Edie let go.

"You were jolly brave, to leap like that," said Edie.

"Brave, but extremely foolish." Aunt Roberta stepped forward and stared down at the three children.

"You could have been killed," said Len Snigson.

"I–I know it was foolish," Gus stammered. "Only I couldn't think what else to do." He raised his eyes and looked up at Aunt Roberta. "I suppose we should introduce ourselves. I'm Gus Smith, and this is my little sister, Greta."

Edie watched, hardly daring to breathe. Would Aunt Roberta lose her temper with him? Poor Gus looked as if he could barely swallow. But at least he had got to speak for himself, like he wanted to. No labels or clipboards or lists. Only Greta seemed totally calm, oblivious to the drama. She beamed, giving Aunt Roberta her best toothiest grin. "Hello," she said. "This is Mr Churchill."

"Churchill? It's a chuffin' elephant!" snorted Len Snigson. "Don't you have respect down there in London?"

"Hello, Greta," said Aunt Roberta gently. "Hello, Mr Churchill." Edie wondered if she saw the tiniest hint of a smile.

"If – if you don't want us, we'll get on the next train to Maidbridge as soon as it comes," said Gus.

Aunt Roberta said nothing. She seemed to be thinking. Edie stared up at her, trying to read her face.

"Please don't send them away. I know you've only just agreed to take me on. And that's probably more than enough," she said, her words tumbling over each other as she spoke. "But it would be so wonderful to have company at Three Chimneys." She took a deep breath. "Like you and Fliss and Uncle

Peter did when you first came... We could be just like you – three railway children!"

Edie felt this really would be a wonderful thing – like borrowing a brother and sister of her own for a while. "What do you think, Aunt Roberta? Oh, please say yes. Please say they can stay..."

Chapter Four

Three Chimneys

"Come along then, children." Aunt Roberta picked up Greta's suitcase. She marched past Len Snigson, whose narrow eyes were as wide as the big brass buttons on his porter's uniform. "You can stay tonight, but I'm not promising more than that."

"Really?" Edie beamed. "Oh, that's wonderful. You're a brick!"

"It's very kind of you," said Gus.

"Thank you, Aunt Roberta," cried Greta, running to catch up with her.

"She's not *your* aunt," hissed Gus. But if Aunt Roberta had heard, she didn't seem to mind. Edie and Gus picked up their own cases and followed her through the waiting room before she could change her mind. All three children were still wearing their gas masks slung around their necks. Not that Edie could ever imagine needing them here: the air smelt so fresh and clean. As she stepped out of the station, she saw a sleepy cluster of cottages with spring flowers in the window boxes and a little village church beside a burbling stream.

"It's beautiful," she breathed, putting her bag down for a moment to look both ways up and down the quiet, hilly street. "Even prettier than I'd imagined." She looked above the little houses towards the rolling moors beyond. "And wilder too," she said with a tingle of excitement.

She reached down and picked up her case again, beginning to regret that she had packed so many of her favourite books. Whichever direction they were going, it was bound to be uphill.

"Here. Let me help. That looks heavy." A figure stepped out of the shadows at the side of the lane.

Edie jumped backwards. She almost screamed. Greta grabbed her hand. Gus slunk back too.

"Sorry." The man blinked. Or at least, one eye did. The other seemed to be made of glass. He tried to smile, but only one side of his mouth moved. The other side – with the glass eye – drooped downwards. The skin on his cheek was tight and shiny, like polished leather on a new pair of shoes. It was scored with three thick scars. "I startled you."

"No, sir!" blundered Gus.

"Not at all," Edie added, but she wished she'd said nothing. Her voice came out far too loud. She might as well have taken one look at the poor man and run away screaming, for all the good her pretence at calmness did now. She tried her best not to stare, at least. Greta, on the other hand, was gawping with her mouth wide open. She took a step closer with her head on one side.

"What happened to your face?" she asked. "Did a tiger fight you?"

"No," said the man. "I'm afraid it was a shell."

"A shell?" said Greta. "Like a seashell?"

"Shh!" Gus pulled her backwards by the hood of her coat.

"Children," said Aunt Roberta. "This is Peter."

"Uncle Peter?" Edie gasped.

"Hello. You must be Edie." He held out his hand. "No prizes for guessing that, though it's been a while since I've seen you." He gave her that same half smile. "You're the spitting image of Phil – or Fliss, as you call her!"

"Gosh!" Edie blushed. "I don't think so. Not really. . ." She was starting to gabble. She did so very much want Uncle Peter to like her. She didn't want him to think that she was the sort of silly girl to be frightened by a few old wounds. She knew, of course, that he'd fought all those years ago in the Great War when he was practically just a boy, but she'd never expected he'd still bear terrible scars like this. Why had no one warned her? She swallowed and tried to take a breath. "What I mean to say is Fliss is so . . . oh, I don't know . . . *elegant*. And I'm not."

"Phyllis? Elegant? Do you hear that, Bobbie?" Uncle Peter snorted. "You should have seen her when she was your age, Edie. She tripped over her bootlaces about ten times a day. I used to tease her that she'd trip up going down the aisle to get married. Then her husband would trip over her trailing laces too and smash his nose in." He looked at Aunt Roberta. "And what was it she used to say?"

"I don't remember." Aunt Roberta stiffened and picked up Greta's suitcase again.

"Yes, you do," said Uncle Peter. "She said she rather marry a fellow with a smashed-up nose than not marry anyone at all."

"Well, she didn't, did she?" said Aunt Roberta firmly. "She didn't marry anybody, as it happens." Her gaze flicked to Edie.

In that split second, Edie saw a cloud cross her aunt's face. Her heart sank. She had no doubts now. She *was* the reason why Aunt Roberta and Fliss had fallen out. Aunt Roberta's anger at Fliss was definitely because she had not been married when Edie was born. The sharp comment and the look of displeasure on her aunt's face had said it all.

Edie turned away, squinting into the sun. She could feel Gus staring at her. For someone who didn't like sharing his own family business, he was certainly hanging on every word now.

"Poor old Phil! She has plenty of choice of husbands, though," laughed Uncle Peter. "If it's smashed-up fellows she's after, we're two a penny nowadays." Edie looked up and he smiled and winked at her with his one good eye. Suddenly he didn't look scary at all. He looked like a cheeky schoolboy, stirring up trouble with his big sister.

Edie smiled shyly back at him.

"Now, how about you introduce your friends?" he said. "I'm sorry I didn't come into the station to meet you. I... Well, to be honest, I find it all a bit noisy with those great big trains."

"Fire-breathing dragons!" agreed Edie as he shook hands with Greta and Gus as she told him their names. Then he picked up Edie's suitcase.

"Here, how about you give me that one too," he said to Gus. As he stepped forward, Edie noticed that he had a limp on the same side as his bad eye and drooping mouth. "I expect you'll all want to run up the hill and stretch your legs a bit after being stuck in a cramped train carriage for so long."

Gus looked for a moment as if he might be too proud to let the old soldier take the case from him. But Edie tugged his sleeve. "Come on!" She felt certain it would offend Uncle Peter to say no. And he was right: she did want to run. After all that sitting around, she wanted to charge up the hill like a galloping horse.

"You can't miss Three Chimneys," said Uncle Peter. "It's the little house at the top of the ridge, just past the stone stile by the old fir tree.

Edie glanced at Aunt Roberta.

"Go on, then!" she said. "It'll do you good." And the three children ran.

Three Chimneys was exactly as Fliss had described it. The little stone house stood in a sunny meadow on the brow of the hill, with the railway line winding away below. The house wasn't big or grand, but it was very pretty. It had little square windows that caught the sunlight, a long, low roof and, of course, the three tall chimney pots which gave it its name. The station was out of sight, but Edie could see a great bridge with tall arches running across one end of the valley and, in the other direction, the yawning black mouth of a tunnel. "Like a dragon's cave," she whispered, holding her sides and trying to catch her breath from running.

"Is this our new home? For all of us?" panted Greta.

"Yes," said Edie. "I hope so."

She had a stitch and she was tired and muddy from racing up the hill, but at least she was better off than poor Mr Churchill. He had been dropped in a puddle along the way and Greta was holding him by his soggy trunk. Together, they all flopped down on the grass. Edie closed her eyes and let the warm late-afternoon sun tickle her face. Even Gus let out a contented sigh.

Nobody said anything for a while. Edie wasn't even sure if she might have drifted off, when suddenly Greta gave an excited cry.

"Look!" she squealed. "There's a llama."

"A llama?" Edie sat up and blinked. A hairy white creature, tethered to a long metal chain, was munching dandelions beside them.

Edie smiled. "That's not a llama," she said. "It's a goat." Even she knew that – although she couldn't remember ever having seen a goat in real life before.

"Oh!" Greta seemed to think about this for a moment and then shrugged. "Lovely llama," she said, as if she didn't care a jot what anybody else thought it might be.

Gus raised his eyebrows. "Papa painted her an animal alphabet all around our bedroom in our old house. L was for llama, you see."

"And what about G?" Edie giggled. "No goats?"

Gus shook his head. "Gorilla!"

"E was for elephant," said Greta. "And P was for—"

"Piglet?" guessed Edie.

"Yes!" Greta cheered with delight. "A little pink one with a curly tail."

"Liar!" said Gus. "It was a porcupine."

Greta stuck out her tongue. "It can be a piglet if I want it to."

Edie sensed another argument. Perhaps this is what it would have been like if she'd had a brother or sister too.

"Your father must be very clever to paint something like that for you," she said, hoping to divert them.

"Oh, he is." Greta gave Edie her most serious stare. "He builds bridges and things for the govern-or-ment," she stumbled.

"Government?" Edie smiled. "He must be very important. But I thought you said he flew planes?" She looked at Gus. "In the RAF?"

"He does." Gus stood up and brushed the grass from his knees. "He used to build bridges, that's all. When he was an engineer. Before. . ."

"Ah," said Edie. "I see." The war had a habit of changing everybody's lives, but Gus seemed eager for the conversation to be over.

"Come on!" He grabbed Greta's hand and pulled her up too. "Let's see who's brave enough to stroke this llama. . ."

"A llama?" The children heard a sharp laugh and turned their heads.

A boy on a delivery bicycle had peddled up the track to the house. Their three suitcases were squeezed into the big basket on the front. "Give over. That there's no llama, London-lad," he puffed. "It's a—"

"A goat! I know," said Gus, his face turning bright red. "I was just playing a game with my little sister."

"He's a beautiful, beautiful llama," said Greta, spinning in a circle and curtseying to the goat as she held the edge of her skirt.

"Stop mucking around now," hissed Gus. "You're making idiots out of us all, Greta."

"City folk, eh?" The boy caught Edie's eye. He grinned and his freckled nose wrinkled with mischievous laughter. Edie could tell at once that he wasn't being unkind. He was only teasing them.

"Hello. I'm Edie," she said, holding out her hand. "Thank you for bringing our cases."

"Albert Perks," he said. "It's no bother. Your uncle told me about your visit. I couldn't let him take this lot all the way up the dale." The boy's warm

Yorkshire accent seemed as friendly to Edie as his sparkly brown eyes.

"Albert Perks?" she said. It was the same name Aunt Roberta had mentioned. "Like the old porter . . . at the railway station."

"Oh, aye," said Albert. "You've heard of him, then? When your aunt and uncle were little'uns. Your ma too, I shouldn't wonder?"

"That's right," said Edie delightedly. "They all thought the world of Mr Perks." Fliss had told her about him many times: how the friendly porter always made them feel welcome at the station.

"Albert Perks was my grandfather," said Albert proudly. "My dad's an Albert Perks too."

"Goodness," said Edie. Her head was starting to spin a little. "Doesn't it ever get confusing? All of you being called Albert Perks, I mean."

"No." Young Albert Perks shrugged. "My grandpa's dead. Three years ago, come Christmas."

"I'm so sorry," said Edie. She wished she'd never asked, but Albert shook his head.

"He had a good innings. And Dad's off at the war just now. He's in the navy. So I'm the only Albert Perks around for a while. Head of the family." He grinned proudly. "Not that they call me Albert Perks, mind. They call me Perky."

"Oh, that suits you," cried Edie. "Perky" seemed such a perfect name for the chirpy, sandy-haired boy. He hadn't stopped smiling since he'd peddled up the lane.

"Hello, Perky," said Greta, grinning back at him with her own gap-toothed smile. She introduced herself, then held out her elephant too, of course. "This is Mr Churchill."

"Oh, aye!" Perky chuckled. "Grand to meet you all." He glanced towards Gus, who hadn't said a word.

Edie leapt in. "That's Gus. Gus Smith."

"Oh, aye!" said Perky again. Gus barely glanced up. But Greta tugged at Perky's sleeve.

"What about the llama?" she said. "What's his name?"

"Stone the crows!" Perky fell off his bicycle in a mock faint. The whole thing toppled over and the suitcases went flying.

"Careful!" cried Gus. But Perky took no notice.

"First of all, that llama is a *GOAT*!" he bellowed, clutching his head in a show of despair. "And, I'll trouble you to notice, *he* is most definitely a *SHE*." He pointed to the enormous udder hanging between the nanny goat's legs.

"Oh, dear!" Edie giggled. But Greta looked deadly serious.

"All right." She plonked herself down on the grass beside Perky. "What's *her* name, then?"

Perky sat up. "I don't rightly know. You'll have to ask your aunty."

"Nurse Roberta is not our aunt," said Gus.

But, just at that moment, the adults came into view at the top of the hill. Uncle Peter was leaning heavily on Aunt Roberta's arm.

"Aunty Roberta! Aunty Roberta!" cried Greta, leaping to her feet. "What's the llama's name. . .? I mean, the goat?"

"Erm. She doesn't really have a name," said Aunt Roberta, looking a little stunned. "We've only had her a week or two, since the ministry cleared her papers. She's a nanny goat. We use her for milk."

"Well, she ought to have a name," said Greta. "Everybody has a name."

"Quite right," agreed Uncle Peter.

"I know!" cried Edie excitedly. "How about Mr Hitler?" It seemed like a very funny name for a goat. But there was a terrible silence and everybody stared at her. "I mean, if the elephant is called Mr

Churchill. . ." she said weakly. "And Greta did think the goat was a boy."

"A boy *llama*!" said Perky, his eyes twinkling again.

"In that case," said Uncle Peter with a grin, "Mr Hitler will do nicely!"

"Oh, Peter," sighed Aunt Roberta. "We can't call our nanny goat 'Mr Hitler'! Whatever will people say?"

"They'll say that our Mr Hitler is the finest nanny-goat-llama for miles around," answered Uncle Peter with a bow.

"Yes, they will!" cried Greta. "She's a darling! Aren't you, Mr Hitler?" She ran and kissed the goat on top of her head.

Mr Hitler bleated and even Gus laughed.

Aunt Roberta turned her back on them all. Edie wondered if she was smiling again too.

"Welcome to Three Chimneys, children," she said, and she pushed open the blue front door.

Greta dashed inside and Gus followed after Uncle Peter. Edie hesitated on the doorstep. She waved to Perky as he peddled away. Then she stood very still. She didn't know why, but she felt she wanted to be alone, just for a moment. She listened to the babble of voices inside the house as she looked down across the green fields towards the railway below.

It could not have been more different from the flat on Glasshouse Street where Edie had lived alone with Fliss her whole life. Yet it all seemed so familiar. She felt a sense of belonging, as if she was coming home. Perhaps it was all those memories Fliss had shared. She felt as if she was stepping into the pages of an adventure story she had read a hundred times before. But it was more than that.

"This is a new story," Edie whispered, hugging herself tightly. "This is a new adventure. And it's mine."

Chapter Five

The Railway Children Return

When Edie woke up the next morning, something felt very strange. At first she couldn't think what it was, but, as she lay listening to the chatter of birds, she knew. For the first time in months, she had slept the whole night through. A deep, relaxing, burrowing sleep, uninterrupted by the drone of bombers overhead or the wail of the air-raid siren.

Her body felt light. Even on nights when they hadn't had to take shelter in the Underground station or the Café de Paris, Edie never slept through until morning in London. Something always woke her, and her body was always stiff with worry, waiting and listening. Now she stretched her arms, feeling like a hibernating bear waking up from a long, deep, lovely rest. The war seemed as if it was a thousand miles away from Three Chimneys.

She rolled over and looked at the little wooden bed beside hers. Greta was up and gone already. But Edie couldn't bear to move. Not yet. She pulled the patchwork quilt up under her chin and felt the delicious warmness of where her body had lain. This had been Aunt Roberta and Fliss's room when they were girls. Gus had an old maid's room along the landing. Peter still had his own childhood room, and Aunt Roberta was now where Edie's grandmother would have slept. The house hadn't belonged to the family then, they had only rented it, but Aunt Roberta bought it after the Great War. She'd been a nurse in France and had come here to look after Uncle Peter when he came home from the fighting.

As quickly as she'd thought she wanted to lie still all morning, Edie was suddenly desperate to be up and exploring. She leapt out of bed, pulled on her clothes and thundered down the stairs, almost tripping on the uneven hobbly-bobbly old steps.

"Morning, sleepyhead," laughed Uncle Peter, who was washing up at the kitchen sink.

"Morning." Edie glanced at the clock. Nearly nine already. How could it be so late?

"Roberta's gone to Maidbridge," Uncle Peter explained. "To see what the Evacuation Board has to say – about the Smith children and whether they can stay."

"Oh, I do hope they can," said Edie.

"Me too. They're nice kids," said Uncle Peter. "Although there's been a bit of a kerfuffle already this morning. Your aunt insisted on washing that grubby elephant."

"Oh, dear!" Edie looked out of the kitchen window and saw Mr Churchill pegged to the washing line by his trunk.

"Young Greta wasn't too happy about it, as you can imagine." Uncle Peter dried his hands. "Now, what can I get you for breakfast? We've got plenty of eggs from our chickens." Edie's mouth fell open as he pointed to a bowl of speckled hen's eggs beside the range. Since wartime food rationing had begun, a box of exotic Turkish delight wouldn't have seemed half so rare and precious as those eggs in London. "And there's some bread and goat's milk, of course. And a good dollop of last year's blackberry jam. "

It was a feast. But Edie glanced at the clock again, desperate to be outside. There was somewhere she wanted to go.

"Itchy feet?" Uncle Peter smiled. "Why don't you just take a slice of bread and run?"

"Can I?" Edie beamed. But before Uncle Peter could answer, the garden door was flung open and Greta hurtled through it.

"Mr Hitler's eating Mr Churchill and she won't let go," she cried.

"Pardon?" It took Edie a moment to realize what was going on. But as she glanced out the window, she saw the nanny goat standing on her hind legs, chewing the elephant on the washing line. At that moment the pegs gave way and Mr Hitler charged off with Mr Churchill swinging from her mouth.

"Oh, dear!" cried Edie.

"Sounds like a job for the War Office," said Uncle Peter, calmly taking Greta by the hand. "Come on. We better go and sort this out. Grab what you want and off you go," he called over his shoulder to Edie. "We'll see you later."

"Thank you." Edie picked up a slice of bread and ran out of the door. She was halfway across the meadow when she saw Gus sitting under a tree looking gloomy. For a moment she thought she might ignore him and pelt past without a word. Part of her wanted to go where she was off to alone. A secret mission! But he looked so lonely and sad that she changed her mind.

"Come on!" she called. "Follow me!"

"Where to?" he asked, not moving.

"Don't ask questions, soldier. It's an order!" she barked, in a bossy sergeant major voice. "You never know," she added. "It might be fun."

Then she ran on. She couldn't wait any longer. It was up to him if he followed or not.

She heard his feet thumping behind her on the meadow grass and, a moment later, he caught up. They ran side by side in silence until Edie stumbled and he caught her by the elbow.

"So, where *are* we going?" he asked.

"You'll see," said Edie, and she skidded to a stop beside a long wooden fence which ran along the side of the railway line. "What's the time?" She grabbed

Gus's arm without waiting for an answer and pulled up his sleeve to look at his wristwatch. It was very fancy, she noticed. A proper man's watch, made of gold with a dark leather strap.

"It was my grandfather's," Gus mumbled.

"It's beautiful," said Edie. The word *Kienzle* was written across it. That sounded German. Or maybe Swiss. The Swiss were famous for making watches, Edie remembered.

"Ten past nine! Perfect!" she said. "If the timetable is still the same."

"What timetable?" said Gus as she let go of his wrist and he scrambled up on to the fence beside her.

"The train timetable, of course," said Edie. "We're waiting for the 9.15 to London."

"Why? You're not running away, are you?" he asked. Then, without waiting for an answer: "If you want to catch a train, you'll need to go to the station."

"I know that, silly," she sighed. "And we're not waiting to catch a train – we're waiting to wave to it."

She explained how Fliss, Aunt Roberta and Uncle Peter had always waved to the 9.15 to send love to their father.

"I'm going to do the same. I'm going to send my

love to Fliss," she said.

"But she's not in London. She's in the ATA. She could be anywhere. . ."

"Up in the sky – flying. I know," said Edie, beginning to regret that she had brought him with her after all. "Oh . . . just wait and see. . ."

There was a rumbling sound which made them look along the track to their right. The dark mouth of the tunnel she had seen from the house opened itself in the face of a rocky cliff. A train burst out of it with a shriek.

"It's the 9.15! The Green Dragon," cried Edie, leaping up and down. She was so excited, she almost forgot to wave. Just in time, she looked up her sleeve and pulled out the clean handkerchief Aunt Roberta had left neatly folded on top of her clothes. Edie wished it had a squirt of her mother's Chanel perfume on it.

"Send my love, Green Dragon!" she roared. "Send my love to Fliss – wherever she is!"

Then Gus was waving his hankie too. "Send my love to Papa," he croaked.

"And from Greta," said Edie, nudging him in the ribs.

"And from Greta!" he said.

Three young servicemen in blue RAF uniforms

were hanging out the window of their carriage. They looked up and waved as they roared by.

"Send our love," the children cried and one of the airmen saluted, although Edie knew he probably hadn't heard what they were shouting. The roar of the train was far too loud.

Then, just as suddenly as it had come, the Green Dragon was gone – thundering on down the line. All that was left were a few last wisps of smoke melting into the clouds.

"See?" said Edie, leaning as far back on the fence as she dared and staring up at the sky above her. "That's our love, floating away. It's searching for Fliss and your papa up there in their planes."

Then she blushed, feeling suddenly silly. Had she gone too far? Would Gus tease her now? He'd probably make some horrid comment about soppy girls.

But he didn't.

"Thank you for bringing me," he said. "This was a good idea."

"Same time tomorrow?" said Edie with a smile. "We can bring Greta too."

"As long as the Evacuee Board let us stay." Gus sighed.

"They will! Aunt Roberta will see to it," said Edie,

swinging her legs. She was sure no one – not even the Pied Piper – would dare to argue with Aunt Roberta, she seemed so firm and sure of everything.

Edie dug in her pocket and pulled out the slice of thick white bread she had taken from the kitchen. It was a little squashed now, but still fresh and soft and delicious. "Wanf sum?" she asked, waving the bread at Gus with her mouth full.

He shook his head. "I already had two fried eggs. Do you know what I'd really like, though?"

"No." Edie swallowed. "What?"

"An apple," said Gus. "You know, picked fresh off a tree. I've never done that in my whole life – not in the city."

"Me neither," said Edie. "There aren't many apple trees in Piccadilly Circus."

"Well, we're in the country now," said Gus, jumping down from the fence. "Come on – Operation Apple! Let's go and find ourselves a great big juicy one."

"Isn't that stealing?" asked Edie, even though her mouth was watering at the thought of delicious ripe fruit.

"It's just scrumping," said Gus as they began to wander along the side of the fence, following the railway line. "That's what it's called when you pick apples off a farmer's tree. It's different. Only sort-of half stealing. All boys in the countryside do it. Or at least, they do in every book I've ever read."

"I know," said Edie. It was exactly the sort of thing Just William would do. "And they always get chased by a furious farmer with a pitchfork. It never ends well."

"That's just for the story, silly," said Gus. "You know, to make it more exciting."

"All right then," agreed Edie. "Operation Apple it is!" She couldn't believe the change that had come over Gus. All his gloominess was gone. She didn't know if it was waving to the train to send his love to his father that had done it, or just the country air. But she wasn't going to complain. She liked this adventurous new Gus so much more than the grumpy one from yesterday, and she felt more wild and plucky herself out here in the country too.

"What we need is a farmhouse," she said. "Then there's bound to be an orchard close by."

But, as they wandered along the edge of the track, there was no sign of any farmhouse, just a pretty patchwork of green fields edged with stone walls.

"Look," said Edie as the railway cutting dropped

away beneath them like the sides of a steep canyon. "There's another tunnel."

"A long one by the look of it," said Gus. "Shall we peep in?" Without waiting for an answer, he climbed the fence, sat on his bottom and half-slid, half crab-walked down the steep bank.

Edie followed, wishing she wasn't wearing a stupid skirt. No wonder it was boys in books who always had the best adventures. They didn't need to worry about their knickers showing.

By the time she reached the bottom, Gus had already disappeared inside the mouth of the tunnel.

"Careful!" she shouted. "Don't go on the track!"

"I won't!" he called, his voice echoing back to her. "But, goodness me, it gets dark quickly."

Edie poked her head around the edge of the bricks and saw his black shadow silhouetted a few steps away.

"What's it like?" she asked, edging forward.

"Damp." His answer echoed back to her. "And cold."

He was right. After only a few paces the warmth of the spring sunshine was gone. It was hard to walk in the pitch black, crunching across the rough stones at the edge of the track. "Ouch!" She tripped on a sleeper and banged her shin on the edge of the sharp metal rail.

She wanted to reach out for Gus's hand, but she thought that might make them both feel stupid.

"Shall we go back?" Gus asked after a few more steps. The light from outside was growing dimmer. "It might go on for miles, for all we know."

"Good idea," agreed Edie, turning around to lead the retreat. "We could always come back with a torch some other time."

"Definitely," said Gus. He sounded just as relieved as her to escape for now, and they both stepped out, blinking, into the sunshine.

"Let's cross over that bridge," suggested Edie, pointing back down the tracks a little way. "We might be able to see a farm from the other side. And if not, we can just walk home that way and go over the level crossing by the station."

"All right," agreed Gus.

Sure enough, as they crossed the narrow footbridge, they saw a tangle of barns and a big white farmhouse in the valley below. Just to the left of it were six or seven stubby trees behind a wall.

"There!" said Edie. "That might be an orchard."

"Are you sure you still want to help me?" said Gus.

"Of course," said Edie with a determined nod. Part of her was already feeling like a coward for turning back in the tunnel. If she wanted a real adventure, she would have to go out and find it.

Chapter Six

Scrumping in Springtime

"Oar's ead arm?" whispered Gus, reading the words off a lopsided sign nailed to the gate. "What sort of name is that?"

"I think it's supposed to be *Boar's Head Farm*," hissed Edie, pointing to the rusty shadows where the extra letters must have once been before they dropped off.

Close up, the farm buildings and the house looked far scruffier than they had from the top of the hill. There were piles of old tin and crates and boxes everywhere. It smelt too – of something thick and wet and sour. The stench made the back of Edie's throat sting.

"Is that manure?" she asked.

"Pigs!" said Gus, as if he was an expert. But Edie couldn't see any animals anywhere, except a half-bald cockerel pecking in the mud.

"Let's follow the wall," she whispered, beginning to regret coming here at all. "We can get into the orchard that way. We don't need to go anywhere near the farmyard."

Gus nodded and they crept towards the ragged group of trees.

Edie scrambled over a section of wall where the stones had fallen down and beckoned to Gus to follow. They dodged past rusted farm machinery and stood beneath the nearest tree, staring up into the branches.

"Are you sure these are even apple trees?" asked Gus, peering into the crisscrossed tangle of twigs.

"I never said they were." Edie shrugged. There was certainly no sign of any fruit. "Why don't you get up there and investigate?" she said, goading him a little.

"The daring heroes in those books you like always climb the trees, you know."

"Fine!" Gus pulled himself up on to the lowest branch, hanging over it with his waist. He was stuck there like a swimmer at the edge of the public baths, paddling hopelessly with his legs in mid-air. "Give me a heave up, then," he yelped.

Crack! Edie hadn't even touched him when the branch snapped clean away from the tree and broke with a sound like a whip. A flurry of shrieking pigeons shot into the sky.

"Yow!" Gus landed on his bottom in a patch of weeds. "That hurt!" he yelped.

Somewhere in the tangle of sheds around the farmyard, a dog started to bark: a big dog, by the sound of it.

"Come on!" Edie grabbed Gus's hand and pulled him to his feet. "Run!" But it was too late.

A great black dog with a head as fat as a pumpkin was lumbering towards them, its tongue hanging out between razor-sharp teeth. A short plump woman barrelled after it, waving her arms and shrieking. "Get off my land!" she yelled, her red face as round and fierce-looking as the dog. "Get 'em, Rex!"

The dog snapped at their heels. It was so close,

Edie could almost feel its hot breath on the back of her bare legs.

"What are you kids doing up 'ere?" roared the woman. "Poking around, I'll warrant."

"We didn't mean any harm," panted Edie, scrambling over the wall. Her stupid skirt got caught on a stone and she was stuck for a minute, halfway up and halfway down the wall, struggling to find a foothold. She pulled her leg free just in time, as the dog circled beneath her snarling.

"We were scrumping for apples, that's all," she tried to explain.

"Scrumping?" As Edie glanced back, she saw the woman's face had turned purple. She had a feeling she'd said the wrong thing. "Donny!" the woman hollered. "Donny! Get your gun!"

Donny? Edie was over the wall at last. Gus landed on the lane beside her. Wasn't Donny the name of the horrible young farmer who'd kicked the crate of chickens across the station platform?

"Run!" Edie cried. There was only one direction to go – and it was straight uphill, of course. Gus pelted after her, stumbling up the steep slope towards the railway line.

Partway up, Edie fell. As she staggered to her

feet again, she looked back and saw the tall, skinny farmer standing on the wall. He was shaking something that looked like a thick black stick at them.

Crack! A sound like another breaking branch split the air.

"Hell's teeth!" gasped Gus.

Edie screamed. She knew it wasn't a stick the farmer was shaking, nor the sound of a breaking branch. He really *did* have a gun, and he was firing it at them.

"Quick!" They had reached the railway line. Gus grabbed her hand and they half-ran, half-rolled down the steep siding and dashed into the deep shadowy safety of the long tunnel they had explored before. Edie didn't mind the dark now, and she didn't feel silly holding Gus's hand, either. They stumbled on, until the light at the end of the tunnel behind them was no bigger than the bulb of a torch.

"Stop!" panted Edie, clutching her aching sides with her free hand. "I think we're safe now. Surely he won't come this far in."

"You're right," puffed Gus, letting go of her hand and doubling over in the gloom. "We must be nearly through. Look. I can see daylight." He straightened up again and pointed towards a small glowing light coming from the other end of the tunnel.

"No!" Edie raised her head and blinked in horror. "That's not daylight," she cried. "It's moving. It's coming towards us."

The tracks beneath them began to hum, almost buzzing at first. Then the tunnel was filled with a great roaring and rattling sound.

"It's a train!" screamed Edie. "Get flat against the wall."

She leant back and almost fell. Where she was expecting solid brick, there was nothing behind her at all. No wall – just an empty space.

"Quick!" Gus grabbed for her. All he got hold of was her pigtail but he pulled.

"Ouch!" yelped Edie. Both of them stumbled backwards into the emptiness, which turned out to be a hollow archway in the tunnel wall.

"It's a manhole," shouted Gus. They were pressed together so tightly he was hollering in her ear. "For the railway workers to. . ." But his words were lost. The roar and shudder of the passing train drowned out everything. There was a great blast of hot air. The tunnel shook and rumbled like an earthquake. Edie thought her ears would burst. Her nose and throat were full of thick, bitter smoke, and as each carriage passed, the lights inside flashed like bolts of lightning.

Then it was gone. The red lamps on the back of the guard's van rumbled away down the long tunnel. The air around them stilled. It was cold and damp and dark again.

"Crikey!" said Gus. His voice was thick and shaky.

"Crikey indeed," whispered Edie. She could barely get her voice to work at all.

Without another word between them, they stumbled back towards the light at the mouth of the tunnel where they'd come from.

As they reached the entrance, Gus paused.

"What if the farmer's still there?" he asked.

"I don't care," said Edie. All she wanted to do was see the daylight, feel the sun on her skin and breathe in fresh air.

"Ey up! What's happened to you?"

Edie and Gus had followed the railway along the other side and come up on the lane behind the station.

They were sitting on the sunny bank, catching their breath, when Perky rode past on his bike.

"You look like a pair of chimney sweeps," he

laughed, turning his bike in tight circles in front of them.

Edie looked at Gus properly for the first time since they had come out of the tunnel. His face was black with soot. She ran her fingers down her own cheek and saw that they were smutty too.

"Oh, dear," she groaned.

"That's good, that is," laughed Perky. "The two sweeps from Three Chimneys. Where's the little'un? Did you leave her up on the rooftop with a brush?"

"Oh, shut up, will you," growled Gus, rubbing at his face with his sweater. But that only seemed to spread the soot around and make things worse.

"Greta's safe at home," said Edie. "But, oh, Perky. It was terrible. We were running away from Boar's Head Farm and we hid in the long deep tunnel and a train came."

"Boar's Head?" Perky stopped circling his bike at last. "The Snigson place? What the dickens were you doing up there?"

"We were just – erm. . ." Edie had the distinct feeling she shouldn't admit to Perky exactly what they had been up to. Something about their whole country adventure was beginning to feel a little silly.

But it was too late. Gus folded his arms and jutted

out his chin. "We were scrumping," he said defiantly. "That's what!"

"Scrumpin'? Oh, dear. That's good, that is! Scrumpin'! It's only springtime!" Perky was howling with laughter. "You won't get apples on trees at this time of year, you daft beggars. Not till the tail end of summer." Edie thought she saw actual tears rolling down his cheeks. "Don't you city kids know nothing?"

"No!" Edie started to laugh too. "It seems we don't!" She could see the funny side. They really had been idiots. Even she knew, now she thought about it, that the trees had to blossom first, long before they could bear fruit.

"There aren't even any apple trees at Boar's Head," chuckled Perky. "Blackthorns, more likely." His face creased up with laughter all over again.

"All right, you've had your joke," said Gus furiously. He leapt to his feet and began pacing up and down. "It's not that funny."

"No," said Perky. "It isn't." And in an instant his cheeky smile was gone. "You need to watch yourselves. Len and Donny Snigson are as bad as folk get. You don't want to go poking around their farm looking for trouble."

"A woman saw us too," said Edie.

"Ma Snigson." Perky nodded. "She's their mother. Runs the farm with Donny since her husband died. Don't let that pudgy apple-dumpling look of hers fool you. She'd slice you up with the wood axe quicker than a leg of ham."

Edie shuddered. "She set her dog on us. Then Donny fired a gun." Her hands were still shaking. She'd thought life in the country would be quiet and peaceful after all the bombing raids of the Blitz. Now, she wasn't so sure.

"You've had a lucky escape," said Perky. "Those Snigsons don't like anyone to go poking their noses round. Folk say they've got all sorts up there: pigs the ministry don't know nothing about, black-market food, fighting cockerels – you name it. But nobody can ever prove a thing."

"I'd like to try," mumbled Gus. But Perky shook his head.

"They're slippery brutes, those Snigsons," he said. "There's Donny up to goodness knows what out there on the farm. And Len – he's the older brother – down here at the station. I think he's probably shifting all sorts of stuff in an' out when he shouldn't be. It's the perfect cover for a porter."

"How terrible," gasped Edie. Could it really be true that the Snigson's were busy trying to cheat the country out of precious food and money just to make a profit for themselves while there was a war on? She found it hard to believe. Especially while brave men like Perky's father – the real station porter – were away fighting.

"It's so unpatriotic," added Gus.

Perky shrugged. "At least Colonel Crowther's got his eye on 'em." He pointed down the lane to where they could just make out the side of a pretty white house with a thatched roof. "He lives there at England's Corner. He's chief of the local Home Guard – it's not a real army or anything, just old farmers and a couple of young lads who haven't been called-up yet. But they've still got a few real weapons and whatnot in case Hitler invades and decides to set out over the dales."

Edie giggled at the thought of the German army marching past the village post office. She was sure Hitler had more important targets in mind. But Perky seemed deadly serious for once. "Colonel Crowther's a real hero. He won medals in the last war and everything. He made the Snigsons join the Home Guard so they'd keep out of trouble. There's only so much he can do, mind, unless he catches the beggars red-handed."

"We should report Donny for what he did today," said Gus. "That would be a start. Surely you can't go firing guns at children? Even in the countryside?"

"Well," said Perky, "maybe, but. . ." He bit his lip. "I don't know. You *were* trespassing."

"Oh, let's not," said Edie. She thought of all the fuss there'd be. On their very first day at Three Chimneys too. And it wasn't even certain Gus and Greta could stay yet. "We were trying to steal apples, after all."

That set Perky off again, howling with laughter. Gus scowled and muttered under his breath, "Country bumpkin!"

Perky stopped laughing. "What's that you say, city boy?" He clenched his fists and stepped forward menacingly. "Shall we see if you can take it on the chin?"

"Come on, then!" Gus put his hands up too like a boxer, although he didn't look half as sure of himself as Perky.

"Oh, for pity's sake!" Edie sighed and stepped in between them. "I don't know about fighting cockerels, but you boys are far worse. We're supposed to be on the same side. There's a war on, remember."

"True enough!" Perky shrugged and the cloud lifted from his face as quickly as it had come. "Friends?" he said, and he held out his hand to Gus.

Gus said nothing. He kicked at the ground, still brooding, his forehead furrowed like a ploughed field. He really did seem to hate being laughed at.

"Come on!" Edie threw her hands in the air. "Haven't you got any sense of fair play, or whatever it is you boys are always going on about on the cricket pitch? Slap him on the back and tell him he's a fine fellow or something and we can all be done with it." Edie knew there was no answer Gus could give back to that.

"Fine!" He wiped his sooty palms on the back of his trousers and shook hands with Perky at last.

"Well," Perky smiled. "Now that's all sorted, I'd best be heading on my way or else my aunty Patsy in the post office'll have my guts for garters." He pointed to the bike. "I help out, sometimes, delivering parcels and telegrams an' that. I was only supposed to nip out to old Miss Peckitt's. She left her ration book on the counter and I said I'd drop it off and be back in a jiffy." He spun the bike around and pedalled away. "Best wash the soot off your faces before you head up home," he called over his shoulder. "There's a pump at the bottom of Colonel Crowther's garden. He won't mind."

Edie looked at Gus's sooty face and sighed. "Perky's right," she said. "We should clean ourselves up a bit. It'll be easier not to have to explain anything when we get home. There's no need to mention running into the tunnel or any of this, don't you think?"

"Of course. I wouldn't want to worry your aunt and uncle," said Gus. Though Edie was pretty sure he just didn't want to get into trouble either.

They slipped through a little white gate, marked ENGLAND'S CORNER, at the bottom of the garden which Perky had pointed out.

They were surprised to see an old gentleman, fast asleep on a deckchair in the sun. He had a battered pith helmet, the sort that jungle explorers wear, resting on his chest. It rose and fell with every breath.

"What should we do?" hissed Edie, frozen to the spot. This was the second time today she had found herself trespassing and she hadn't even had her lunch yet. "Should we wake him up and ask permission to use the pump. Or should we just turn back and tiptoe away?"

"No need for either course of action, young lady."

The stretched-out figure spoke. "I am not sleeping, my dear. Merely dozing." He raised his head a little and peered at them over the top of the pith helmet. "You must be Peter and Roberta's niece. Edith, is it?"

"Yes," she replied and nodded. She didn't dare to say she'd rather be known as Edie. His voice was so rich and round, he sounded more like someone off the radio than an ordinary living person. It was as if he was making an announcement about her on the BBC.

"And this, I presume, is your evacuee friend," he continued. "The jumper-from-trains? I've heard all about you."

"He's Gus," said Edie. "Gus Smith... Introduce yourself," she hissed in Gus's ear.

"I don't need to now. You've done it already," Gus hissed back.

"Quite so." Colonel Crowther sat up and Edie saw that he had the most wonderful bushy moustache. It curled up perfectly, like the handlebars of a bicycle, at both ends.

He must look magnificent with his full Colonel's uniform on, helmet and everything, she thought.

"So," he said, "you wish to avail yourselves of my pump?" He peered at their sooty faces. "I can quite see why."

"May we?" asked Edie. "Perky – I mean Albert Perks, the young one – said you wouldn't mind and . . . well, as you can see, we've got ourselves in a spot of bother."

"Say no more!" The colonel raised his hand. "Any friend of young Perky's is a friend of mine." He motioned to an old-fashioned iron pump beside the hedge. "Help yourself."

"Thank you!" Edie gratefully began to scrub her face.

"No doubt you were scrumping or some such larks?" The colonel chuckled.

"Yes, sir." Gus nodded. "You see," he whispered in Edie's ear. "He doesn't think it's stupid to try scrumping at this time of year. And he's a colonel. . ."

When they had both washed their faces, Colonel Crowther saluted them. "That old damson tree will have some fine fruit in a few months' time," he said pointing towards a sunny corner of the house. "Come and help yourself, if you're still around."

"Thank you," said Edie. "That's very kind."

With their faces clean and their pride restored a little, she backed out of the garden at England's Corner. The Colonel seemed so upright and grand, she felt almost as if she had met King George himself.

Chapter Seven

Headquarters

When Edie and Gus got back to Three Chimneys, they found that Aunt Roberta had just returned from Maidbridge too.

"Good news," she said. "I spoke to the Evacuation Board and Gus and Greta can stay here for the duration of the war if they need to. They are now our official Three Chimneys evacuees."

"Oh, that's wonderful." Without thinking, Edie threw her arms round Aunt Roberta. She was so excited, and it was such a magnificent thing she had done, that she almost forgot to be scared of her. If Aunt Roberta could welcome the evacuees so generously, perhaps she could come to truly love Edie too, and the whole row with Fliss would be forgotten.

Aunt Roberta returned Edie's hug just as warmly, and Edie felt a glow inside.

"Thank you! Now we can be the Railway Children after all," she cried. She slapped Gus heartily on the back and blew a kiss to Greta. Already, she couldn't imagine living here without them.

"Hooray!" cheered Greta dancing round and round the kitchen table. "Three Chimbleys is going to be our home."

"Thank you, ma'am," said Gus, a little formally.

"Oh, goodness, if you're going to stay, I think you ought to call me Aunt Roberta, don't you?" she said.

"Thank you, Aunt Roberta." Gus grinned and Edie felt like throwing her arms around her all over again.

"The board were finding it hard to place evacuees as it was," Aunt Roberta explained. "Most city children came in the first few months of the war – and half of them have gone back to London already, thinking the bombing down there wasn't going to be nearly as bad as it is. The whole thing seems to be a bit of a muddle." Aunt Roberta shrugged. "But that still leaves the question of school."

"School?" Edie had almost forgotten about that.

"Gus is too old to go to the one in the village," said Aunt Roberta. "And you will be too by the end of term, Edie. So I suggested Uncle Peter and I could teach you here until the summer holidays. Then we'll think about you both starting at the grammars in Maidbridge in September. We'll sort something out for Greta then too – if this rotten war is still going on, that is."

"So you mean, no school this term at all?" said Edie. "The summer holidays start now?"

"Well, as I say, you'll still have some lessons with Uncle Peter and with me when I'm not working at the hospital," Aunt Roberta repeated. "But. . ."

All three children were dancing round the kitchen table now, whooping and cheering.

"I wouldn't be so excited if I was you." Aunt Roberta raised her voice above the noise. "I'll have you all learning poems by heart, you know!" Then she rolled up her sleeves and went outside to milk the goat.

"Isn't she manificent?" whispered Greta.

"Magnificent?" Edie laughed. But she had to agree, there was something rather magnificent about Aunt Roberta. She was strict and firm and proper. So different from Fliss. But she was also kind and generous. Every once in a while, Edie caught a glimpse of the girl she must have been all those years ago – the young Bobbie who'd had the wonderful idea of saving the train by ripping up her red flannel petticoats.

"Petticoats!" Edie cried aloud. "That reminds me."

"What are you talking about?" Gus looked at her as if she was mad.

"You'll see!" said Edie, and she ran out of the door after Aunt Roberta. "I was just wondering," she called, "you don't have any old trousers I could have, do you? Small ones, that is?"

"Trousers?" Aunt Roberta looked confused.

"Yes. Like the Land Girls wear, when they work on the farms," said Edie. "It's just that now I'm going to live in the countryside, I can't run around wearing skirts all the time. It's not practical."

Aunt Roberta smiled. "I'll ask around and see what I can do."

*

Two days later, Aunt Roberta gave Edie her first lesson. It wasn't on the poems of Wordsworth or the sonnets of Shakespeare. It was on how to milk a goat.

Edie found she was quite good at it. It was all about rhythm ... and talking gently to the goat. It was certainly easier than when she'd tried to learn the cello. Aunt Roberta had left her to carry on alone, and she had already got an inch or two of milk in the bottom of the pail, when she saw Perky riding up the path on the big post office bicycle.

"I've summat for you," he called, and Edie's heart leapt.

"Is it a letter?" she cried, almost knocking over the precious milk. Fliss had promised to write as soon as she reached the airbase, but there'd been no word yet.

"Gosh. No. Sorry!" Perky looked crestfallen. "I didn't mean to get your hopes up. It's... Well, actually it's a parcel from my aunty Patsy in the post office."

"A parcel? For me? From your aunt Patsy?" Edie didn't want to sound rude, but... "Why?"

"You'll see!" Perky grinned as he handed over a loosely tied package done up with old newspaper and string. His eyes were sparkling with mischievous delight – a look Edie was beginning to recognize all too well.

"Thank you," she said calmly. She laid the package on the grass and carried on milking the goat. "Good girl, Mr Hitler," she whispered.

"Aren't you going to open it?" said Perky, almost hopping from foot to foot in his excitement.

"Not just now," said Edie vaguely. She had no idea what she was going to find inside, but one thing was sure, she wasn't going to give Perky the satisfaction of opening it in front of him. Not when he was grinning from ear to ear and giggling to himself like that.

Unfortunately, Mr Hitler must have caught sight of the newspaper out of the corner of her eye. As the nanny goat lunged for the parcel, Edie grabbed the pail of milk and saved it just in time. But it was too late to rescue the package. Mr Hitler was tossing it up and down in the air. As the goat munched on the newspaper, two pairs of boys' grey flannel shorts fell out on to the grass below.

"Kegs! I've never seen a girl wear aught like those before!" tittered Perky. "They used to belong to my cousin, Stan. But he's outgrown 'em."

"They're just perfect!" cried Edie. She couldn't have been more pleased if it had been a velvet dress with new shiny patent-leather shoes like the ones Fliss always bought her for the Christmas pantomime. She didn't care how much Perky was laughing. "These are just what I need," she said, picking up a pair of the shorts and holding them against her waist for size.

Gus was cutting across the grass with a saucepan of kitchen scraps for the chickens. Soon he was laughing just as loud as Perky at the sight of Edie holding up the grey boys' shorts and whirling around in delight.

"They're not for a girl," he teased.

"I don't see why not," said Edie, but she suddenly stopped mid-whirl to stare at Mr Hitler who was still munching contentedly.

"Oh, boys," she cried. "It's not funny. I think Mr Hitler has eaten all the newspaper . . . and the string as well."

She watched in horror as the goat swallowed the last dangling strand of twine and belched loudly.

Edie was very worried about goaty Mr Hitler for the next few days. Poor Greta was even more anxious. She asked Uncle Peter (as she and Gus now called him) if they ought to sleep in her stall at night to check she was all right.

"Don't worry. Goats are tough. They can eat anything," said Uncle Peter. "You'll see."

Sure enough, the nanny goat seemed to show no ill effects whatsoever. The following week, she ate an important-looking form from the Ministry Of Food all about milking quotas and rationing.

Edie was delighted there was no harm done, and she was thrilled with her new shorts too. They were especially useful when the children went on adventures, exploring the countryside around Three Chimneys, criss-crossing back and forwards on the bridges over the railway tracks.

Lessons turned out to be few and far between – in fact, there were hardly any at all. Aunt Roberta was only supposed to be a volunteer at the little hospital over in Stacklepoole, but she was such a good nurse she was always in demand. She often set off on her bicycle at the crack of dawn and wasn't seen again until nightfall.

"You must be very busy there," said Edie once.

"Not with anything too serious," answered Aunt Roberta. "It's mostly old ladies with sore feet and bad bunions. But with so many doctors away at the front, I suppose that's all part of the war effort too."

"I suppose so," said Edie. At first, she couldn't

shake the feeling that Aunt Roberta was away so much because she was trying to avoid her, still resentful of the fact that Fliss's illegitimate daughter had come to stay at Three Chimneys at all. But as time passed, she began to feel this couldn't be true. No matter how late Aunt Roberta got back, she always crept upstairs to kiss Edie goodnight. If it was very late, and Greta was asleep, they'd creep back down to the kitchen where Aunt Roberta would make them both a cup of tea and they'd chat about their day. Or, if it was early enough, there'd be a story for her and Greta all tucked up in bed.

Edie soon found herself listening out for the sound of Aunt Roberta's bicycle on the gravel outside whenever she was working late. Those evening chats were often one of the best parts of her day.

Meanwhile, an older girl called Maisie Gills came from the village to help with chores and look after Greta when Aunt Roberta was working. But that still didn't leave Uncle Peter time to teach them lessons either. He was always busy cooking and gardening.

"Digging for victory," as he liked to say, waving his spade in the air. And when he wasn't doing that, he was "tinkering" in the old stable he'd set up as a workshop behind the house. He had made a bit of money as an antique restorer before the war, but what he liked most was collecting old bits and pieces related to the railway and returning them to their former glory. Edie loved watching him shine the brass on an old lamp or wind the cogs to restore life to a dusty station clock. He had boxes and baskets filled with a rusty tangle of springs and wheels and screws – and some things which seemed to have no name at all. It mostly looked like old junk to Edie, but Uncle Peter would hum under his breath, plunge his hand into a particular basket and come out with the perfect penny-sized cogwheel he was searching for.

Every once in a while his hands would shake and he would have to sit, trembling uncontrollably for a moment before he could begin again.

"I wanted to be an engineer when I was a boy," he told her. "But then the Great War came along and . . . well, I never got the training."

It was one of the bad days and his hands were shaking a lot. He kept digging them into his pockets and Edie tried not to stare.

"Go on. Run along outside and play," he said, smiling at her gently. "Otherwise I might just have to set you a test on algebra after all."

Even if there wasn't much schoolwork, the children did have chores: feeding the chickens, milking the goat, collecting eggs, helping to dig and plant in the vegetable garden – anything which could bring in extra food. But once those jobs were done they were free to run and explore and play. Edie had never known such freedom, and the skirts she'd brought from London stayed hanging in the wardrobe as she wore the baggy knee-length shorts every single day.

"Do you know what we should do?" she said excitedly, when they were sitting on the fence above the railway line one afternoon. "We should find a camp, or a clubhouse, or something. That would make it official. We really would be the Railway Children then."

"Good idea," agreed Gus. "Every club needs a meeting place."

"Aye," said Perky, who had finished school for the day and come to join them. "Count me in."

"Can I be in the club too?" asked Greta.

"Of course you can," said Edie.

But Gus raised his eyebrows. "You'd be better off staying at home with Maisie," he said. "Real Railway Children adventures might be too daring for a little girl like you. And you always complain you don't want to walk too far, anyway."

"No I don't," said Greta. "Do I, Edie?" Her lip began to tremble.

"Of course not." Edie could see she needed to act fast before there were tears. "Railway Children for ever!" she said, jumping down from the fence and solemnly shaking hands with each of them in turn.

"Railway children for ever!" the four children agreed.

"So," said Edie, "does anyone have any idea where our clubhouse could be?"

"In a flowerpot?" suggested Greta.

"A flowerpot?" The boys spluttered with laughter.

"I think we'd have trouble finding one big enough to fit us all in," said Edie kindly. She bit her lip trying not to laugh too.

But Greta was deadly serious. "Not me," she said. "I'm a teeny-tiny fairy with silver wings."

"Well, I'm not!" snorted Perky. "But I reckon I know a place which might just do the job. Come on!"

He led them along a path at the side of the railway line.

The boys spread out their arms and pretended to be Spitfires.

"Is that what your dad flies, then?" asked Perky.

"Yep." Gus nodded and dipped away to the left to machine-gun a patch of stinging nettles.

"Which squadron?" asked Perky. "I've got a couple of cousins who work in ground crew – they might know him."

Perky seemed to have cousins everywhere.

"I shouldn't think so." Gus swooped back to give the stinging nettles a second blast. "He's not stationed anywhere near here."

"Nor's my oldest cousin, Johnny," said Perky. "He's down Kent way, somewhere. Maybe he's with your dad!"

"Maybe." Gus circled back for the stinging nettles a third time but seemed to lose heart. His wings dropped and turned back into arms, which swung by his side as he kicked a stone across the tracks. "Actually, I'd rather not say, if you don't mind. It's all a bit hush-hush."

"You mean he's in the secret service or summat?" Perky's mouth fell open in surprise.

"A spy?" cried Edie. "You never told me that!"

"Shh!" Gus glanced up and down the empty track. "That's sort of the point of being a spy," he whispered. "You're not supposed to tell anyone."

"Mum's the word." Perky put his finger to his lips, clearly impressed.

"He flies top-secret missions and stuff, that's all," said Gus. He shrugged and lifted his arms again ready for takeoff.

"My mum flies Spitfires too sometimes," said Edie, seeing as no one had bothered to ask.

"Rubbish!" The boys laughed.

"They don't let women fly Spits," said Perky.

"Of course they do," said Edie, and she stuck out her arms and dive-bombed a patch of brambles.

Greta followed. "Wheeeeeeee! *Boom*!"

"I thought you were a fairy?" scoffed Gus.

"I am," said Greta. "I'm a splitfire fairy!"

"*Spit*fire!" groaned Gus.

"Whoa! Wait till the Luftwaffe hear that!" laughed Perky.

"The Luffy-what?" said Greta.

"They're the German air force," said Edie, although the way Perky had said it in his broad Yorkshire accent, you would never have guessed. "Come on! Let's loop-the-loop. We'll show these boys how it's done."

All four children flew off, noisily making the sound of whirring propellers.

"Here it is," said Perky as they reached a short stretch of straight track, just before the bend and the long, dark tunnel. He scrambled up a high bank with some scruffy-looking trees. From the top, Edie could see a little siding running parallel with the main track. It was all overgrown with weeds and brambles and looked like it hadn't been used for years.

They slithered down and walked along the siding. Half hidden beneath creeping ivy and the branches of a fallen tree was an old train carriage. It towered above them, much taller than any train Edie had ever seen before, as there was no platform running beside the rusty old rails, of course. The bottom of the carriage door was level with the top of Edie's head, so she couldn't see in. It made her a little dizzy to think that trains were always like that – so that you'd actually be stepping out in mid-air if there wasn't a raised platform to catch you.

The old carriage must have been rather grand once, perhaps for first-class passengers. It had rich, chestnut-coloured sides and the remains of what looked like white lace curtains in the windows, though they were ragged and grey now. The glass was mottled with grime and moss was growing in the cracks of the wood. But Edie thought it was just perfect.

"It's like a little house," she cried. "Or a caravan!" She ran around the back of the carriage to the other side. "Look! We can get in from here." A small tree had fallen from the bank opposite, making a sort of drawbridge between the side of the bank and the carriage.

Edie teetered along the fallen trunk and yanked the handle, almost toppling backwards as she pulled the door towards her. "It's open!" she cried, stepping into the carriage. She saw at once that it must have been some sort of dining car or smoking saloon. Faded, greenish-blue seats like armchairs lined each side beneath the windows and little wooden tables were scattered about. One lay like a turtle on its back in the middle of the carriage with only three legs. There was a big brass pot that looked as if it might have once contained a plant, but now had the remains of a bird's nest in the bottom. The little smoked-glass lampshades were thick with cobwebs and dust. It was clear that nobody had been inside for years.

"Oh, Perky," cried Edie, grabbing him by both hands as he stepped inside. "It's wonderful!" She waltzed him round and round, almost tripping over the three-legged table.

"Steady on!" He laughed.

Greta grabbed Gus and made him waltz around the carriage too.

"Wunerful!" she agreed.

"I don't know," said Perky. "There's always the disused signal box on the way to Stacklepoole Junction. That might suit us better!"

"Certainly not!" said Edie, and she flopped down on to one of the huge chairs, sending clouds of dust billowing into the air. "This is the Railway Children HQ, and that's decided."

"What's HQ?" asked Greta.

"Head-Quarters," shouted all three older children at once.

"Everyone needs a headquarters in wartime," Edie explained. "And this is ours."

"I love it!" said Greta, leaping on to the seat beside her and sending more dust billowing into the air.

"I'd be careful if I were you. Reckon there might be rats nesting in that upholstery," warned Perky.

"Rats!" Greta leapt on to Edie's knee.

"Nonsense. He's only teasing," said Edie, glaring at Perky over the top of Greta's head.

"Of course I am," he agreed. And Edie hoped that was true.

"So, what'll we do here anyhow?" said Perky, sitting down too and stretching out his long legs.

"That's easy," said Gus. He was standing down the other end of the carriage, peering out of the window. "We can find out what's really going on at the Snigsons' farm. Look."

Edie went and stood beside him. The bank at the side of the track was lower here and he pointed through a gap in the trees. She saw that they had a perfect view of the field and Boar's Head Farm in the valley below.

"How exciting. We'll be like real spies," said Edie. She had always wanted to be involved in an undercover operation.

"If the Snigsons really are dealing in black-market goods then they ought to be stopped," said Perky. "It's a terrible crime, especially when brave men like my dad are away fighting."

"Exactly!" agreed Edie. "And wouldn't it be wonderful if we were the ones to catch them at it?" She thought how proud Uncle Peter and Aunt Roberta would be.

"I can find us some old notebooks from the post office, if you like," said Perky excitedly. "We can jot down anything suspicious we see."

"Good idea." Edie could tell this was going to be fun. "What we really need is some binoculars," she said. "Then we'll find out what those terrible Snigson brothers are up to for sure."

Chapter Eight

The Dark Demon

Aunt Roberta came home early from the hospital that night. They had a delicious supper of potato pancakes with raisins and a spoonful of sweet heather honey on the top.

"Even the Café de Paris couldn't serve something so scrumptious," laughed Edie. But, as soon as she'd said it, she felt a sudden stab of sadness, remembering the cafe was gone now. Suddenly, she missed Fliss dreadfully. It had been so long since she'd heard from her – why didn't she write and send news?

If Fliss was here now, she'd turn the wireless on and we'd all have a bit of a dance while we did the washing-up, thought Edie.

But no one seemed in the mood to listen to music at Three Chimneys tonight. Edie glanced around the table. Perhaps she wasn't the only one feeling a little glum. Everyone seemed strangely silent for once.

Gus was quiet and thoughtful, but there was nothing unusual about that. Poor little Greta was practically falling asleep in her plate. She must be exhausted from their expedition to HQ. The disused dining carriage was quite a hike for her short legs. But the biggest change was in the grown-ups. Edie realized Uncle Peter had barely said a word since they'd sat down. Aunt Roberta kept glancing at him anxiously, offering tight little smiles of encouragement which Edie couldn't understand.

"Uncle Peter," she said, hoping to lighten the mood a little. "Do you have any binoculars we could borrow?" She wasn't going to mention she wanted them for spying on the Snigsons, of course. That was the sort of thing adults never approved of – even though she was certain they'd all be heroes if they really could uncover a secret stash of black-market food the Snigsons were hoarding somewhere, making money out of the war while people in the cities starved. For now, she planned to pretend that she and Gus wanted the binoculars to do some birdwatching. She was tempted to say they'd seen a golden eagle. Did you get golden eagles in Yorkshire? She wasn't sure.

As it was, Uncle Peter didn't even seem to hear her.

"Uncle Peter?" she said again.

But Aunt Roberta shook her head. "Leave it just now," she whispered. "Uncle Peter's tired. He overdid it digging in the vegetable patch, I think."

Edie nodded as Aunt Roberta stood up and pushed back her chair. "Come on, now. Let's tidy up these plates." She clapped her hands and Uncle Peter flinched.

"What was that?" Edie sat bolt upright in bed in the middle of the night. Somebody was screaming.

"*Help me! For god's sake, help me!*" The voice was shrill and shaking. Then there was a terrible stream of cursing and moaning – a torrent of awful swear words.

Edie was shocked. It was Uncle Peter's voice. What

was wrong? She threw back her covers. But before she could move, the pad of hurrying feet sounded on the landing outside and she heard Uncle Peter's door opening and closing. He screamed again, but this time another voice, Aunt Roberta's, answered. It was soft and soothing, though Edie couldn't make out the actual words.

Edie's heart was pumping as she sat there hugging her knees. She had never heard any grown-up shout terrible things like that before, especially not kind, gentle Uncle Peter. He must have had a terrifying nightmare to make him scream like that.

She glanced over at Greta. She was still fast asleep, her thumb in her mouth and her fingers gripping Mr Churchill's woolly grey ear. How could she have slept through all that noise? The soft yellowy bulb of the electric night light Greta always insisted on was glowing gently between their beds, but the rest of the room was pitch dark from the thick blackout curtains drawn across the windows. Even out here in the middle of the countryside, they weren't allowed to show a chink of light. It would only take one stray German bomber to see a tiny glow and they might just decide to unload one of those deadly bombs on Three Chimneys. Edie had heard they often dropped them anywhere they could on the way back home, just to be rid of the extra weight.

Her heart was still thumping, but the house was quiet again. Uncle Peter had stopped screaming. Edie leant over and turned the night light off. She slipped out of bed and tiptoed to the window in the pitch dark. She lifted the corner of the heavy curtain and saw that there was a pale moon shining over the meadow. She wanted to open the window and breathe in the fresh air, but didn't dare in case she woke Greta with the noise. The latch was stiff and creaky and it always needed a good, hard thump to make it budge. She pulled the curtain tight again and tiptoed back to the bed, stubbing her toe in the dark. She switched the little night light back on and lay down, staring at the ceiling. She was still tense, half-listening out for another cry. It felt like those awful nights in London, where she used lie awake waiting for the air-raid siren to scream.

She closed her eyes and tried counting sheep – that was supposed to make you fall asleep. The trouble was, she couldn't decide what sort of sheep they should be. In London when she'd counted sheep they were always white and fluffy. But that was before she'd come to Yorkshire and realized there was such a variety to choose from. Should they be white sheep or grey ones, black ones or speckle-faces? And should they jump over a gate, or a fence, or perhaps a lovely dry-stone wall like the ones that criss-crossed the fields here? It was no good. She was never going to get back to sleep like this. Her chest felt tight and she was hot and restless.

She slid out of bed, pulled on her dressing gown and slippers, and eased the door open. She stood on the dark landing for a moment, listening. She could see a crack of light under Uncle Peter's door and heard the murmur of voices as he and Aunt Roberta talked. She turned as quietly as she could and crept downstairs. It was pitch dark with the shutters closed and she stumbled for a moment, forgetting the extra little step between the hall and the kitchen. She kicked the empty milk pail over and it clattered across the tiled floor.

"Whoops!" She fumbled for it in the dark, set it upright again, and froze, her heart pounding louder than ever. Would someone shout out? Would Aunt Roberta come down to see what had happened?

She held her breath and counted to a hundred in her head before she dared to move. Perhaps they hadn't heard her after all.

For a moment Edie wondered about just getting a glass of water and going back upstairs. But she felt too wide awake and restless. She'd been scared by Uncle Peter's shouting and she couldn't bear the thought of staying in bed. The night light wasn't bright enough to read by, and she knew she'd just lie there worrying about things. About Fliss. And the war. And poor Uncle Peter now too.

No. She didn't want that. She wanted fresh air. Before she could change her mind, she slipped out through the garden door, darted round the side of the stables and ran across the moonlit meadow. She lost her slippers in the first few steps, but stopped to pick them up, and scampered on barefoot, clutching them in her hand. The moon was bright in the sky, its silvery light clear enough to see by. Everything looked black and white like a photograph to Edie. A bomber's moon, as everyone had always called it on bad nights for air raids in London, because the enemy planes made the most of bright light and the chance to see their targets down below. But she was sure she'd be all right out here in the middle of the countryside.

At first Edie just ran. It felt wonderful to feel so free with the cold night air on her face. But as she reached the bottom of the meadow, she stopped running and put her slippers on again. She picked her way over the stony ground at the edge of the grass. She knew, without having stopped to make the decision, that she was heading to the railway line.

As she slithered towards the fence, her heart gave a leap. There was someone else there, sitting on the railings.

"Hello, Edie," said Gus. He didn't even look round. "I wondered if you'd turn up."

Edie felt a great rush of relief. "Oh, it's you!" she said, still keeping her voice to a whisper. It seemed wrong to talk loudly in the dark. "If I'd known you were here, I'd have brought a midnight feast." She clambered on to the fence and sat beside him. Neither of them asked why the other one was awake.

"Five minutes," said Gus, tapping his watch.

"Five minutes till what?" whispered Edie. "Till midnight?" Perhaps he thought she was serious about the feast.

"Not midnight. We're way past that," he said. "Five minutes until the 4.36. If it's on time."

"4.36?" asked Edie. "How do you how there'll be a train then?"

"Haven't you heard it?" said Gus. "When you're lying in bed at night?"

"No," said Edie. Her voice was growing a little louder now as she got used to being outside with the darkness all around her. "I usually sleep like a log. Except tonight, of course. . ." She trailed off, sensing again that neither of them wanted to mention Uncle Peter and all those terrible things they'd heard him shout. She realized too, from the way he spoke, that Gus must lie awake most nights.

"Have you been out here before?" she asked. "In the dark?"

"No," said Gus.

"Oh, good!" Edie didn't mean to sound so pleased. She was surprised how glad she was. It felt exciting being out here like this and she was happy she wasn't playing catch-up with some adventure Gus had already had.

"Is it just me," she asked, "or is it getting darker?"

"Much darker," said Gus, beside her. She realized she could hardly see his face any more. A thick cloud had passed across the moon.

"Listen," said Edie. "I can hear it." There was the unmistakable *chug-chug-chug* of a train, far away, like a little drummer boy softly practicing a rhythm to get it right.

She glanced down the line, expecting to see lights coming towards them but there was nothing. Just darkness. The noise grew louder – thumping now like a proud drum major in a big brass band.

"Where is it?" she said. But before Gus could answer, a shadow roared out of the gloom. Steam whistled and the train flew past. There were no lights on it at all. Just a red glow from the firebox where the hot coals burned.

Like the flames in a dragon's mouth, Edie thought.

"They don't have lights at night, so the bombers can't see them," said Gus, raising his voice above the noise now as the dark carriages rattled past.

"Of course," said Edie. It was like the blackout, except even more important out here. The Germans were always trying to bomb the railway lines. Nothing could move around the country without trains.

The carriages rattled on and on and on.

"It's like a serpent," she gasped. "The Dark Demon." She had never seen a train so long. Not that she could see it now, of course. She could just make out the shape of the shadows enough to tell that they were not passenger carriages rattling by. The Dark Demon was some sort of goods train, with long low wagons, loaded up with ominous black mounds.

"Bombs," said Gus. "From the munitions factories."

Edie shuddered. She knew they were their bombs. *Good bombs,* she almost found herself saying. But that was nonsense. There was no such thing as a good bomb. She hated the thought of them all – screeching through the air, shattering everything to smithereens below.

Then, with a last rattle of a final wagon, the mighty train was gone.

"Phew!" Edie found she'd been holding her breath and let it out in a rush.

"We never asked it to send our love," said Gus.

"I wouldn't want it to," said Edie. "Not that one. Not the Dark Demon."

"Fair enough," said Gus. There was maybe just the hint of a laugh in his voice, but he didn't tease her. She knew Perky would have done, if he'd been here.

They both sank down and sat with their backs against the fence. Gus had a blanket wrapped around his shoulders and he spread it across their knees.

"We should go back, really," said Edie. But neither of them moved.

"Bit dark still," said Gus, glancing at the sky. "I wouldn't want you twisting your ankle in the long grass." He was teasing her now for sure. "You know how clumsy you are." She couldn't see his face, but she knew he was grinning.

She decided to ignore it. She knew he was only using her clumsiness as an excuse not to go home quite yet. The moon was coming out from behind the clouds again and they probably could have seen well enough to find their way. But neither of them seemed ready to move. She could still hear the sound of poor Uncle Peter's dreadful screams echoing inside her head. It was nice to be out here in the fresh air for a while longer, even if it was a little chilly. Edie pulled the blanket up around her neck and yawned.

"We mustn't go to sleep," she said. "Not here!"

Chapter Nine

The Telegram

Edie woke slowly and pulled the blanket around her, keeping her eyes closed for a last moment of peace.

She had fallen asleep sitting up, and she thought she was back in London with a Tube train rattling past her as she dozed against the wall on the Underground platform at Piccadilly.

It didn't smell like the Underground. It smelt clean and fresh . . . but there was a tang of smoke too.

"Fliss?" She yawned, stretching out her hand, expecting to find her mother beside her.

Then she opened her eyes and remembered where she was. She was on the bank above the railway track. It was light now and the sky was still pink from the sunrise. The dawn air was chilly and the grass was damp with dew. She pricked her ears. The sound she could hear was another train rumbling towards them. Gus was stretching sleepily beside her. He must have fallen asleep too.

They staggered to their feet and she wrapped the blanket around herself, shivering, as the train rattled past. She could see the sleepy early-morning passengers slumped in their seats, some resting their tired heads against the windows, catching a last wink of sleep before the start of a busy day.

"Sweet dreams!" she whispered.

"6.06," said Gus, checking his watch. "What shall we call this one?

"The Dreaming Dragon," said Edie decisively. "Come on. We better get back."

They were about to move off when they heard voices on the other side of the track. A railway porter's hat popped into view above the opposite bank, followed by Len Snigson's head and shoulders.

"Listen, Donny, I'm telling you. It's somewhere here," he said. "From this telegraph pole, all the way back to the mouth of the tunnel."

"Quick!" hissed Edie. It was too late to climb back over the fence, but there was a little bush beside them. She shoved Gus hard, pushing him behind it and crouched down too. Peering through the tangled branches, she could see Len marching up and down the edge of the railway line with his head bent. A moment later his brother Donny appeared too, and they both began to pace together.

"What are they doing?" mouthed Gus.

"I think they're looking for something," she said, leaning towards him to whisper in his ear. She was crouching on her haunches and almost lost her balance as she shifted her weight. She put a hand out to steady herself and a bird shot up into the air, squawking. Edie was so startled, she screamed before she could stop herself. As she leapt back in surprise, she lost her balance completely and went tumbling down the steep bank, rolling over and over, thumping and bumping towards the railway line below.

"Ouch!" She came to a sudden stop as her tumbling body smacked into Len Snigson's big black boots.

"Well, well!" he said, sucking the words through his teeth so it sounded almost as if he was smacking his lips together. "If it ain't the little London rat. You keep turning up like a bad penny."

"I'm not a rat," said Edie, trying to struggle up on to her hands and knees. How dare he talk to her like that? First he'd told her she had lice and now he was calling her a rat.

"'Course you're a rat," said Len. He made no effort to help her up. "Tell her why, Donny."

"I dunno!" His brother just shrugged and stood by looking stupid.

Len sighed. "Rats spy on folk, see. Rats poke about, sticking their greasy little snouts in where they're not wanted."

"That's right!" agreed Donny, picking up his brother's theme at last. The two of them were circling round her, as if she really were a rat and they were yapping terriers determined not to let her escape from a trap.

"Leave her alone!" Gus came charging down the bank behind them.

"A pair o' rats, eh?" Len spat on the rails. "Both spying on us, were you?"

"Honestly, we weren't," said Edie as Gus leapt to

her side. "We were just. . ." She wished they weren't wearing their pyjamas and dressing gowns. That made thinking of excuses rather hard.

"Just what?" laughed Donny.

"We came to watch the trains," she said firmly. "And now, if you don't mind, we'll just go home for breakfast."

She grabbed Gus's sleeve and took two big steps up the bank.

"Ha!" Len let out a snort. "Run along, then. If I see your aunty, I'll tell her you were out at the crack of dawn. She'd want to know."

"That's right. Bairns shouldn't be running around in their 'jamas," added Donny.

"Fine, you tell her," said Edie, but her legs were shaking. She knew Aunt Roberta would be horrified if she knew they'd been out there half the night.

"Leave it," whispered Gus. He was the one tugging her sleeve now.

But Edie spun around again. "I just wonder what it is you're hiding, that's all," she said, staring down on the Snigsons from the safety of the bank.

"We're not hiding nowt," said Donny, scratching his head. Len kicked him.

"Shut up! We don't have to say anything to them. They're only kids."

"Of course you're hiding something," said Edie boldly. She climbed up on to the top of the fence. "Only people who are hiding something worry that they are being spied on."

Then, without waiting for an answer, she jumped down from the fence and walked up the hill to Three Chimneys.

"I'm warning you," hollered Len. "Keep your nose out of our business. Or I'll teach you a lesson you'll never forget."

When the children got home, they found Aunt Roberta had already left for the hospital.

Uncle Peter was sitting at the kitchen table while Greta spooned mountains of sugar on top of her porridge, as if she'd never heard of rationing. Uncle Peter didn't seem to notice. He barely even noticed that they had come in.

"We went for a walk," said Gus hastily.

"In your pyjamas," Greta giggled. "That's silly."

Gus glared at her as he ladled porridge into bowls for him and Edie. But Uncle Peter didn't even look over. He was still wearing his pyjamas too.

Edie accidentally dropped her spoon on the floor with a clatter and he jumped.

"Sorry," she said as he sloshed hot black coffee all over the table. He looked up in utter confusion, and, for a terrible moment, Edie thought he was going to cry. "Here, let me get that." She grabbed a cloth and wiped up the spill.

"I think I might go to my workshop," he said. But he didn't move.

"Good idea. We'll go for a walk," said Edie quickly. "We'll take Greta, if you like." She knew how much she wanted to be alone sometimes, and it seemed Uncle Peter might be best left in peace.

"You've just been for a walk," said Greta.

"And now we're going for another one," said Gus firmly. "And you're coming with us."

He and Edie bolted down their porridge and hurried upstairs to get dressed.

When Edie came down again, Uncle Peter was standing in the hall, holding a battered leather case on a strap.

"You wanted these," he said, opening the lid to show a pair of field glasses.

"The binoculars," said Edie. "Thank you." She didn't even know he had remembered her asking, but they'd be more useful than ever now. After what they had overheard the Snigsons saying this morning, she was in no doubt whatsoever that the brothers were up to no good. She'd love to find them digging up a barrel of stolen whisky beside the railway line or something. That would serve them right for calling her a rat!

"I had the binoculars in the last war," said Uncle Peter. "In France."

"I promise I'll look after them," said Edie, as he handed her the case.

Uncle Peter shrugged. "I don't care if you drop them in the sodding mud."

Then he sat down on the bottom step of the stairs and put his head between his hands.

Edie was shocked. "Uncle Peter. . ." She stretched out her hand towards him but he shook his head.

"I'm sorry. Go for your walk," he said. "I'm not going to be very good company today."

Edie paused for a moment, hating to leave him like this. But he waved her away again.

"Don't worry. I'll be fine. Off you go." He looked up and smiled as best he could.

"What are we looking for?" said Greta for the hundredth time.

"I don't know," Edie answered. They were walking up and down the edge of the railway track, searching for any sort of clues. Edie had the binoculars slung around her neck like the gas mask she always used to wear. None of the children bothered with them any more. Not out here in the countryside.

"We heard him, as clear as day," she said, turning to Gus. "Len Snigson told Donny there was something, somewhere between this telegraph pole and the mouth of the tunnel."

"Black-market goods, I expect," said Gus. "Probably something from the farm. Food, I suppose."

"Sausages?" said Greta, licking her lips.

"Maybe." Edie ruffled her hair. "Let's just keep searching. You never know your luck."

Before long, Greta gave up completely and sat on the bank making a dandelion crown for Mr Churchill, who had come with her, of course.

Gus and Edie took it turns to keep an eye on her or walk further down the line. Five or six times they must have covered the distance between the telegraph pole and the start of the tunnel. They looked along the tracks, up on the bank, under bushes and up trees.

"Never mind a sausage, there's not so much as a bacon rind," said Edie, flopping down on the bank beside Greta. "I give up!"

"Whatever it was may well have been squashed by a train by now," said Gus. He lay down on the grass too and stared up at the sky.

"Oh, dear," said Edie. "Imagine if it was a crate of eggs."

"Look," said Gus after a moment. "There's a plane up there."

"So there is," said Edie, shielding her eyes from the sun. A shape, too big for a bird, was coming this way. She'd got quite used to seeing all sorts of planes flying over in London, but realized this was the first one she'd seen out here in the country. She lifted the binoculars and looked through them. The plane was painted in green-and-brown camouflage with a big propeller on the front.

"Is it one of ours?" she said, feeling a sudden panic. She passed the binoculars to Gus.

"Of course," he said. "It's a Hurricane." He hadn't even looked through the binoculars yet. "I can tell by the sound of the engine."

"Which ones are ours, Gussy?" said Greta, trying to grab the binoculars from him. "Which side are we on?"

"The British, of course," said Gus furiously.

Edie leapt to her feet. "Hello," she called, running

along the top of the bank and waving as the plane flew over them. "Good luck! *Bon voyage!*"

It was far too high and far away for the pilot to hear them, of course. But she imagined for a wonderful moment that it might be Fliss. Maybe she was delivering the Hurricane to an airfield nearby.

They ran after the plane, heading in the direction of the village. As they came up on to the bridge by the lane, they saw Perky. He was standing up on the pedals of his bicycle, shielding his eyes from the sun and staring into the sky too.

"Did you see it?" he said. The plane was no more than a speck in the sky now. "She was a right beauty!"

"I wouldn't mind flying one of those," said Gus. And the boys took it in turns to scan the sky with the binoculars.

Edie smiled; it was good to see them becoming friends. But Greta was pulling on her sleeve.

"I need a wee," she said, jiggling from foot to foot. "And so does Mr Churchill." She waved the knitted elephant in the air.

"All right," said Edie. "I'll take you to the station. You can go to the ladies cloakroom there."

"Hang on a second," cried Perky. "I've got summat

for you, Edie. I was on my way up to Three Chimneys with it when I saw the plane."

"Is it more boys' clothes?" asked Greta.

"No," said Perky. "It's a telegram."

"A telegram?" Edie froze as he held the thin brown envelope towards her. Telegrams meant someone was dead or wounded or missing in action, didn't they? Why would anyone be sending her a telegram?

"Don't look so worried," said Perky. "Telegrams aren't always bad news, you know."

"Not always?" That didn't sound very reassuring. Edie's fingers were shaking as she took the envelope. She couldn't bear to open it. It was silly, but some part of her felt that if she never read the telegram, then any bad news might stay sealed in there and never escape. It was like the Greek myth Aunt Roberta had made her read in the one and only lesson they'd had last week – the one where Pandora had all the sorrows of the world sealed away in a box, just so long as no one peeped inside.

"Do you want me to read the telegram for you?" Gus stretched out his hand.

"No, I don't!" She almost slapped him away.

"I need a wee," whined Greta. "And so does Mr Churchi—"

"Shh!" hissed the boys.

Edie ripped the envelope in one clean movement, unfolded the paper and read it.

Her hands started trembling more than ever.

"What's it say?" asked Perky.

"It says," breathed Edie. "Station. 11.53."

"Station? That must mean this station," said Gus.

"Yes." Edie blinked, trying to stop the tears that were gathering in her eyelashes and threatening to roll down her cheek. "It means Fliss is coming to visit me," she breathed. "She's coming here. Today."

Chapter Ten

Missing

Edie stared at the telegram. 11.53.

"What's the time now?" she asked.

Gus glanced at his watch. "About 11.48, I'd say."

"That's only five minutes," cried Edie. "I've got to go. . . Here. Take these." She handed Gus the binoculars and turned to run. But Greta tugged at her sleeve.

"I still need a wee," she said. "And—"

"—So does Mr Churchill," chorused the boys as she waved the knitted elephant in the air.

"Fine!" snapped Edie. "You better come with me." She grabbed Greta's hand a little more roughly than she meant. She'd much rather have gone to the station alone.

"Why don't Gus and I take the binoculars to HQ? Aunty Patsy said I'd be free once I'd delivered the telegram," said Perky. "We'll see if we can spot anything happening at Boar's Head Farm."

"Good idea. I'll fill you in on what Edie and I overheard this morning," agreed Gus. "And Edie. . ."

"What?" She was already running.

"Keep an eye on Len while you're at the station," he hissed.

"I will," she said, tugging Greta along behind her, but to be honest she wasn't really thinking about the Snigsons now. Len could unload a whole handcart of smoked hams right in front of her and she wouldn't stop him. Not if it meant she could get to see Fliss.

"Come on, Greta. Be quick!" she snapped, helping her to dry her hands in the washroom. She could already hear the train chugging towards the station. She steered Greta through to the waiting room, with its brass umbrella stand, leather seats and pretty bowls of flowers.

"Why don't you and Mr Churchill stay in here and play fancy ladies? Don't move," she said, without waiting for an answer. She wanted Fliss all to herself for a moment. "I'll be back in five minutes."

She dashed on to the platform just as the 11.53 shuddered to a halt, billowing smoke.

A short, dumpy woman dressed all in blue stepped down from the carriage furthest away from the engine and waved to someone. Edie spun round and looked the other way. That certainly wasn't Fliss.

She ran down the length of the train peering into the carriages. Nobody else seemed to be standing up or getting off. Then she spotted a tall, slim figure emerging from the carriage nearest the engine.

"Fliss?" She peered through the smoke. But as the figure stepped forward, it turned out to be Reverend Greaves, the vicar.

"Hello, Edie; see you on Sunday, I hope."

"Yes." She wheeled round and glanced along the carriages again. An elderly man was hobbling towards the level crossing. Out of the corner of her eye, she noticed Len pushing a perambulator along the platform. He must be helping a mother down from the train. It was hardly anything to report to HQ.

"Cooee." The plump lady was still waving. "Edie? Edith? Is that you?"

"Me?" It took Edie's brain a moment to connect. The plump lady was waving at *her*. She was wearing a blue ATA uniform just like the one that Fliss had. "Yes," she said slowly. "I'm Edie." But where was Fliss?

The whistle blew and the 11.53 chugged out of the station. As the smoke cleared, Edie saw there was nobody else on the platform but the two of them now.

"Hello, dear." The jolly-looking ATA lady held out her hand. "Belinda Barton-Withers. I fly with Fliss. Did you get the telegram?" she asked. Then she slapped herself on the forehead, almost sending her smart blue cap flying on to the railway track. "Of course you got the telegram or you wouldn't be here."

"Yes," said Edie, trying to hide the disappointment in her voice. "Isn't Fliss coming herself?" Then she had a sudden moment of panic, like when she'd first seen the telegram in Perky's hand. Perhaps this woman, this Belinda Barton-Withers, was here to break the bad news gently. "She is all right, isn't she?"

"Lawks, yes! Fit as a fiddle," assured Belinda. Edie felt her whole body relax. Fliss was safe! But as quick as her fear subsided, it was followed by the crushing disappointment that she hadn't come. She was so sure the telegram had meant Fliss would be here.

"Shall we take a pew?" Belinda tapped the sunny bench at the edge of the platform, inviting Edie to sit down. "I'm on my way for a few days leave with my family. When Fliss heard I'd be passing through, she asked if I'd have time to get off the train and send you her love and all that. I've only got ten minutes; I need to be back on the 12.04."

"That's so kind of you," said Edie. She tried to keep her voice bright, but was sure it must sound hollow and flat.

If Belinda noticed her disappointment, she didn't show it. "Fliss says she's awfully sorry she hasn't written yet," she boomed. "The censors read all our letters anyway, so she can't say anything really juicy. But if she gets the chance to fly an old crate over Yorkshire, she's going to make a detour to Three Chimneys and do the best damn beat-up you've ever seen."

"Beat-up?" Edie was finding it hard to work out half of what Belinda Barton-Withers was saying. It wasn't just that her voice was so hearty and posh; she kept using phrases that Edie didn't understand.

"Sorry, old thing." Belinda clapped Edie on the

back, almost sending her skidding off the bench. "Beat-up is ATA slang. It means to fly a plane really, really, low. So low, you can pretty much see the pilot's lipstick." She laughed. "All the girls do it if we get a chance to fly near home. It's very frowned upon by the Top Brass, of course. If Fliss had written about that in a letter she certainly wouldn't have been allowed to send it to you."

Edie smiled. She could imagine Fliss loving the exhilaration of flying low and waving out of the cockpit. It did sound exciting – though horribly dangerous.

"Your mother's a terrible daredevil, of course! One of the worst," said Belinda, making Edie's tummy clench. "She likes flying the small speedy planes, like Hurricanes and things."

"We saw a Hurricane today," cried Edie. Perhaps it wasn't too silly to think it might have been Fliss after all. Although, if it was, she'd surely have done the daring beat-up Belinda had described and swooped low over the whole length of Three Chimneys meadow.

"I prefer flying a Halifax myself," said Belinda. "You know, the big heavy bombers. It's a bit like driving a winged tank..." And she began to explain all the different sorts of planes the women got to fly. They were often up at the crack of dawn, delivering aircraft all over the British Isles, collecting them from factories or taking them to airfields whenever the fighter pilots and bomber squadrons needed them.

Before Edie knew it, the next train was chugging into the platform and it was time for Belinda to continue her journey north to see her family.

"Let me give you a hug," she said, launching herself at Edie and throwing her arms around her neck. "I'll pass it on to Fliss when I get back."

Edie was half-smothered by Belinda's enormous bosom, but she didn't care. "Send her so much love, please," she begged. She had been so disappointed at first, but now she wished the visit didn't have to end. If Fliss couldn't come herself, then Belinda Barton-Withers was the closest she could get. There were so many things Edie hadn't asked. Things about Fliss and her life in the ATA.

"I almost forgot," cried Belinda, leaning out of the window as the train began to move. "She asked me to give you this." She held out a bar of Fry's chocolate. Edie could see Fliss's familiar bright-red lipstick kiss on the wrapper. It brought a lump to her throat.

148

She raced along beside the moving train and caught hold of the chocolate bar just in time.

"Thank you for stopping off!" she called, waving until she couldn't see Belinda waving back any more. Then she swallowed hard, dried her wet eyes and walked back along the empty platform to collect Greta from the waiting room.

She slipped the chocolate bar into her pocket. She'd keep it as a surprise treat to share as they walked home. Greta deserved it. She had been so good, staying in the waiting room all this time, instead of coming out to run up and down the platform like Edie had thought she would. She felt rotten she'd been so impatient with her earlier.

"Greta," she called, pushing open the waiting room door. "I'm sorry I was so long."

But the waiting room was empty. Greta wasn't there and Mr Churchill was lying all alone by the umbrella stand.

"Greta?" Edie's heart began to race. She grabbed the elephant and ran out of the station to the street outside. She looked both ways up and down the hill. But the road was deserted. "Greta, where are you?" she cried.

Edie stood outside the station and shouted as loud

as she could but there was no answer. How could a village be so quiet? There didn't seem to be a soul out and about. Edie dashed across the road and peered over the stone wall beside the river.

Surely Greta wouldn't have gone down there? She dangled over the wall and looked in both directions. There was no sign of anything except the burbling water and the mossy, slippery rocks. The river had always looked so pretty. Now it just seemed wide and cold and dangerous.

"Greta?" Edie ran back towards the station. She checked the washroom and lay down flat on her belly so that she could see underneath the chairs in the waiting room. Perhaps Greta was playing hide and seek? But if she was, she definitely wasn't hiding anywhere inside.

Edie ran on to the platform. "Hello?" she cried. "Is anybody here?"

Where was Len Snigson? Surely he was supposed to be on duty? There was no sign of the porter or anybody else on the station at all.

Edie was about to charge out on to the road again when she stopped and tried to think clearly.

Take a deep breath, she told herself. She knew for certain that Greta was in the waiting room when the

11.53 arrived because she'd left her there and run out to the platform to meet the train. . .

"Oh, why didn't I let her come with me?" Edie wailed out loud. She took another deep breath and tried to concentrate. Greta definitely hadn't come on to the platform while Edie was talking to Belinda Barton-Withers on the bench. She would have spotted her if she had, she was sure of that. Unless. . .

"The trains!" gasped Edie. Could Greta have got on to one of those?

Surely I'd have noticed, she thought. But she knew it wasn't true. She was so busy looking for Fliss the first time and saying goodbye to Belinda the second, that anything could have happened. Greta might have slipped on to either one of those trains unseen.

She could be halfway to Scotland by now! thought Edie desperately.

But even if that was true, one thing still didn't make sense. If Greta had got on the train for fun – for an adventure – she would definitely have taken Mr Churchill with her. She would never leave him behind anywhere. Edie couldn't bear to think what that meant.

She hugged the elephant tightly, breathing in a sweet mix of barley sugar, cod liver oil and Lifebuoy soap. It was exactly how Greta smelt when she climbed into Edie's bed for a cuddle in the mornings.

Edie wanted to stay calm, but as hard as she tried, she couldn't escape from the terrible thought which was hammering inside her head: if Greta's beloved toy was still here, did that mean someone had snatched her and taken her against her will? If someone had kidnapped the little girl, she might have dropped Mr Churchill as they bundled her away. Edie couldn't imagine any other reason why Greta would ever leave him behind – not even for a moment.

She sank down on the bench behind her, her legs shaking so hard she could barely stand up. She took another deep breath and forced herself to think logically. Who else had she seen on the platform since she first arrived?

"Len Snigson," she whispered. The last time she'd noticed him, he was unloading the big black pram from the 11.53. She couldn't remember seeing him on the station at all since then. Surely he should have been there to help with the 12.04? Edie clutched her tummy. Could Len have taken Greta? It didn't seem possible. He might be a bit of a crook, happy to sell black-market goods and profit from the war. But would he steal a child? Would he hurt her? Surely not.

Then Edie remembered how she'd goaded the porter this morning, saying she would get to the bottom of the Snigson's secret activities. His warning rang in her ears: "*Keep your nose out of our business, or I'll teach you a lesson you'll never forget.*"

Why hadn't she kept her mouth shut? What if the Snigsons were up to something truly awful – something they would do anything to keep secret?

Edie struggled to her feet.

Had Greta paid a terrible price, all because Edie had been snooping?

She gathered Mr Churchill into her arms and ran. She had to find Greta before it was too late.

Chapter Eleven

The Pig Club

Edie grabbed Mr Churchill by the trunk and ran out on to the station forecourt. The row of little cottages above the railway line showed no sign of life. Edie's legs were still shaking as she tried to think what to do next. The nearest police station was all the way in Maidbridge, so that was no good. But if she ran up hill towards the village shops there would surely be someone who could help her. She might even see PC Bevan on his bicycle.

Edie had only taken two steps when she changed her mind. Perky had told her once that PC Bevan was married to the Snigsons' older sister, Enid. Perhaps he couldn't be trusted to help.

"England's Corner!" she gasped. She skidded round and pelted downhill, in the opposite direction. She should have thought of it at once. The pretty white house was just around the bend in the lane. Colonel Crowther was head of the Home Guard. He could probably have his troops out searching for Greta within minutes. He might even have the authority to radio the signal boxes further up the line and have the trains heading north stopped and searched.

"Colonel Crowther!" she bellowed, banging the brass lion's head knocker as loudly as she could. "Colonel Crowther, are you home?" She thought she saw a flicker of movement behind the downstairs curtains and pressed her nose against the window to peer through the glass. She was surprised to see how drab and bare it looked inside. There were only a few sticks of battered-looking furniture and an old iron trunk for a table – not at all what she would have expected from the grand brass knocker outside and the pretty roses growing up the walls.

"Hello?" she called. But there was still no answer. It must just have been a shadow from the sun she had seen moving. She pounded the knocker again and stood stock-still, listening with her head on one side, praying for the sound of footsteps coming to the door. But there was nothing.

Edie was furious with herself. She had wasted more time than ever now. "What an idiot!" She should just have gone straight to the village high street in the first place. There would have been plenty of people there.

As she thundered back up the hill, she saw the church straight ahead of her. For a wild moment Edie thought about running in and ringing the bells. That was only supposed to happen if there was an enemy invasion. The bells didn't even ring on Sundays any more. They had been silenced until the war was over except in the case of dire emergency. But this was an emergency – a real one. If Edie rang them, everyone would know she needed help. She had no idea how to ring a bell, of course. But they'd surely make some sort of clanging noise if she pulled on the long dangly ropes at the bottom of the spire.

Then she remembered Reverend Greaves. Of course, she had spoken to him at the station earlier too. Perhaps he'd seen Greta. He might even have taken her back to the vicarage for some orange squash. Mrs Greaves, the vicar's wife, ran the village playgroup. Greta had gone with Maisie Gills last week.

Edie was about to cut across the churchyard when she heard the sound of crunching gravel on the lane behind her. A bicycle! She spun round, thinking it might be PC Bevan on his rounds. But as the cyclist came into view, she saw that it wasn't the policeman riding up the lane.

"Aunt Roberta!" She'd never been so pleased to see anyone in her whole life. The feeling of relief made her knees go weak. "Thank goodness you're here," she cried, leaping out into the middle of the lane so that Aunt Roberta nearly skidded into the ditch. Edie was so glad to see her, and so frightened about what might have happened, she didn't even worry about getting in trouble for losing Greta in the first place.

"I was at the station with Belinda Barton-Withers. And when I went back to the waiting room, it was only Mr Churchill there," she gabbled. Edie was still clutching the elephant and she waved him under Aunt Roberta's nose. "I think Len Snigson's kidnapped her!"

"Slow down, Edie," said Aunt Roberta, laying a hand on her arm. "What are you talking about? I just passed the Snigson brothers in the lane."

"Where?" cried Edie. She grabbed the handlebars of the bicycle as if she was ready to leap on and start pedalling.

"They were by the crossroads arguing loudly about something they'd mislaid. But Greta wasn't with them, Edie. I don't know what you mean, accusing them of kidnapping her."

"Perhaps she's escaped," gasped Edie.

"Who? Greta?" Aunt Roberta raised an eyebrow.

"We were spying on the Snigsons this morning," said Edie. "I know we shouldn't have been but ... well, Len vowed he'd get his revenge on us. And then I went to the railway station because there was a telegram. And I told Greta to stay in the waiting room. But she didn't. And now she's in terrible danger. Either Len Snigson has kidnapped her, or she's on a train to Scotland all alone. . ."

"How odd," said Aunt Roberta. She didn't sound in the least alarmed to hear that her young evacuee was in such awful peril. "Only, isn't that Greta over there?"

She pointed towards the churchyard.

"Where?" Edie stood on tiptoes and looked

over the wall. She couldn't believe her eyes. Aunt Roberta was right. Greta was standing amongst the tombstones, clutching a bunch of wilted daffodils in her arms.

"Dear me," said Aunt Roberta. "She's taking flowers off old Bob Widdop's grave. He's only been buried a fortnight. . . Stop! Put those back, Greta! You mustn't do that."

Greta looked up, her eyes wide with innocent surprise. "Oh, hello."

"Greta!" cried Edie, charging across the churchyard. "I thought you were lost. Or kidnapped. Or dead. . ."

"All right, Edie," Aunt Roberta warned, running to catch-up. "There's no need to be quite so dramatic. As you can see, Greta seems perfectly all right. We don't want to give her nightmares, do we?"

Greta didn't seem in the least disturbed. In fact, she scooped another bunch of flowers from a grave and trotted away up the path.

"Where are you going, young lady?" said Aunt Roberta. "Put those flowers back, this minute."

"I can't," Greta called over her shoulder. "I need to feed my babies." And she disappeared around the side of the church.

"Her babies?" Edie and Aunt Roberta looked at

each other. "What is she talking about?"

They peered around the building and saw Greta posting daffodils one by one under the hood of an enormous black perambulator.

"I saw that pram," cried Edie. "At the station. Len Snigson was unloading it from the 11.53."

"Heavens," said Aunt Roberta. "I think Greta might have done a little bit of kidnapping for herself. . ."

"You mean. . ." Edie glanced around the empty churchyard. There was certainly no sign of any mother or nanny in charge of the pram. "You don't think there's an actual baby in there, do you?" But even as she spoke, she saw the big black pram rocking from side to side. There was definitely something inside it.

"Eat up," cooed Greta, feeding yet more daffodils under the hood.

"Greta," said Aunt Roberta gently. "May I have a look at your lovely baby?"

"Of course." Greta beamed with pride as Aunt Roberta and Edie both stepped forward. "But it's not a baby, it's—"

"—A piglet!" gasped Edie. A pair of beady black eyes looked up at her and a pink snout was poking out from amongst the daffodils in the pram.

"Not just one piglet, silly," said Greta. "It's twiglets. . ." She pushed the flowers aside and there was a squeal as a second little piggy popped its head up above the blue crocheted baby blanket. "Sorry. Not twiglets. . ." Greta giggled. "I mean twin piglets! See?"

"Yes," Aunt Roberta sighed. "I do see."

"They're adorable." Edie couldn't help smiling as the piglets snuffled and snorted. In all the excitement she'd almost forgotten to be cross with Greta, although her heart had only just stopped pounding.

"Did you find them like this at the station?" she asked. No wonder poor Mr Churchill had been forgotten. Greta did always say she wanted a piglet of her own. Now she had stumbled upon two . . . in their very own baby carriage.

"I pushed them here all by myself," said Greta proudly, cooing as she rocked the pram. "They were hungry. That's why I'm feeding them daffodils. Piglets like daffodils."

"How extraordinary. Who would leave piglets in a pram?" said Aunt Roberta.

"Len Snigson, that's who!" said Edie triumphantly. "I told you I saw him unloading it from the train. At the time, I didn't think much of it. I thought he was helping a mother and there must be a baby inside."

"Hmm." Aunt Roberta looked thoughtful. "The only reason to hide piglets in a pram is if they're not supposed to be there," she said. "The ministry certainly won't be aware of these little fellows, that's for sure."

"Black-market pigs! Maybe that's why the brothers were arguing," said Edie excitedly. "I expect they were planning to smuggle the piglets up to the farm. I bet Len was meant to sneak them off the train and meet Donny at the crossroads. Only he turned his back for a minute. Then Greta came along and. . ."

"And it turned into the case of the vanishing piglets!" said Aunt Roberta with a little smile.

"Can we keep them?" said Greta. "Please. . ."

But before anyone could answer, Edie put her finger to her lips. "Shh!" she hissed. "Look!" She pointed towards the wall.

Len Snigson's head had popped up over the top. But it disappeared again just as quickly.

Aunt Roberta cleared her throat. "Why don't you come out and show yourself?" she said firmly. "It appears we may have something you are looking for."

"Oh, er . . . that's our old pram, that is." Len's head appeared again. His face was as flushed and pink as the piglets he was trying to hide. "It's – er – got sentimental value, that's all. . ."

"Oh," said Aunt Roberta. "I assumed it was what was inside the pram that was of interest to you."

"What's that you say? There's summat inside?" Len had climbed over the wall. "Piglets? Well I never," he said, peering into the pram as if he had never seen them in his life before. "How the dickens did they get there?"

"How indeed," said Aunt Roberta. "Are they your piglets, Mr Snigson?"

Edie could see a little muscle in the side of Len's cheek pumping away as he tried to think of a good answer.

"Yes, Nurse Roberta, ma'am," he said at last. "They're our piglets."

"Then what are they doing in a pram?" said Edie.

Len scowled at her. His cheek was pumping again.

"Donny was playing a trick on me," he said at last. Edie could imagine the cogs inside his brain whirring. "Yes, that's it!" He smiled now as if he had finally settled on a good story. "It tickled our Donny no end. Leaving the piglets in the pram like that. He knew I'd go and peep. I'm right soft when it comes to babies, you know."

Edie found that very hard to believe. This story was getting more and more unlikely by the minute. Even she knew that wartime food rationing meant every farm animal was supposed to be accounted for to the ministry. But the Snigsons were clearly breaking the law. These piglets were smuggled, Edie was sure of it.

"Imagine my surprise," said Len, "when it wasn't a bairn sleeping in there, but a pair of porkers. . ."

"And the piglets are definitely yours?" repeated Aunt Roberta. "From the farm, I mean. They haven't just arrived by train or anything?"

"No. They're definitely our piglets," said Len boldly. "In fact I – er – I ought to be getting them back to Donny right away. They'll – er – need food and that."

"I've fed them," said Greta crossly. "They like eating flowers."

Len ignored her. He stretched out and took the handle of the pram.

"Stop! You can't take them." Greta tugged at his jacket and tried to pull him away.

"Now, Greta." Aunt Roberta raised her eyebrow. "Mr Snigson is quite entitled to take his own pigs away. Stand back, please."

Greta's lip was shaking as Len barged her aside and began to push the enormous perambulator away. He was almost running with it down the path towards the church gate.

"Ta very much, Nurse Roberta. Sorry about all the confusion." He looked back over his shoulder and smiled like an innocent choirboy.

Edie couldn't stand it. He was getting away. "You're not actually going to let him take them, are you?" she hissed. Surely Aunt Roberta knew the pigs weren't really from his farm, no matter what he tried to say?

"Just one last thing, Mr Snigson. . ." Aunt Roberta raised her voice. Edie wasn't sure but she thought she saw her aunt wink. "You do have all the relevant papers for them, I presume?"

"Papers?" Len was squirming again. "I'm sure we do. I'll – er – I'll have to ask Donny. Now if you'll excuse me, I ought to be getting back to the station."

While he was talking, Aunt Roberta had walked round to the front of the pram and was blocking the path.

"I tell you what we'll do," she said brightly. "We'll hold on to the piglets until you can find the papers. That way I won't have to report it to the ministry. You know, of course, that smuggling black-market animals while there's a war on is an offence you can go to prison for." She paused and folded her arms as if to let this sink in. Len kicked at the ground with his boot.

"Of course, if you can't find the piglets' papers, we could always raise them for you at Three Chimneys," said Edie with a cheeky grin.

"Exactly. We'll start an official pig club for the whole village," added Aunt Roberta.

"You can't do that!" snarled Len.

"I think you'll find we can," said Aunt Roberta firmly. "Come along, girls. You can push the pram up the hill."

"Hooray! We get to keep the twiglets... I mean piglets!" cheered Greta. But Len grabbed Edie's arm as she squeezed past him with the pram.

"Now look what you've done! Meddling in my business again!" He gripped her shoulder but Edie shrugged him off.

"Any time you've got the papers, we'll gladly give the piglets back," called Aunt Roberta, climbing on to her bicycle as Len slunk back to the station, like a dog with its tail between its legs.

Edie puffed as she pushed the pram up the hill. Greta was no help at all. She just kept dancing to the hedgerow and back again with Mr Churchill in one hand and bundles of grass to feed to the piglets in the other.

Aunt Roberta had taken the daffodils away. She said they might make the poor things feel sick.

"There's just one thing I don't understand," wheezed Edie, as they reached the stile by Three Chimneys at last. "What's a pig club?"

"It's something for the whole village," Aunt Roberta explained. "We've no idea where these piglets really came from. It's not fair that our family should profit from them any more than the Snigsons should. If we start a pig club then everyone can have a share. They can all send their kitchen scraps to feed them up nicely and then the whole village will get something when it's time to. . ."

"Oh, I see," said Edie quickly. She put her finger to her lips as she glanced at Greta, skipping along beside the hedgerow, looking for the juiciest blades of grass to feed to the little piglets.

"You mean when it's time to turn them into b-a-c-o-n and s-a. . ." Edie trailed off. She couldn't quite remember how to spell sausages. And the thought was too horrible.

"There's no point in being squeamish," said Aunt

Roberta firmly. "There's a war on. You children will have to face the facts. As soon as these little piggies are nice and fat, they'll be turned into juicy. . ." Aunt Roberta trailed off too. She glanced at Greta, who was leaning into the pram, singing lullabies to the "darling Twiglets", as she insisted on calling the little twin pigs.

". . . Into juicy p-o-r-k?" asked Edie, with her eyebrow raised.

"Exactly," Aunt Roberta sighed. "I don't like to think about it either, really," she admitted. "But don't worry, we'll have the whole summer to enjoy with them first. We won't do anything until Christmas."

"And maybe the war will be over before then, anyway," said Edie. Anything seemed possible here in the peaceful countryside. Len Snigson had met his match in Aunt Roberta. Greta had been found, safe and sound. And Belinda Barton-Withers had brought news of Fliss too. As she joined in singing lullabies to the sleepy, snuffling Twiglets, Edie suddenly felt a great wave of fresh hope. Just for a moment, she felt herself relax.

It seemed as if nothing really bad could ever happen. Not while she was here at Three Chimneys.

Chapter Twelve

Secret Codes

The Snigsons never did turn up with the proper papers, of course, and the young pigs settled in well. Two old milk churns were left in front of the post office in the village and anyone with vegetable peelings or other leftovers could donate them to the pig club. Colonel Crowther kindly offered to drive the churns up to Three Chimneys in his motorcar whenever they were full.

Everyone referred to the twin piglets as the

Twiglets, of course. Although, when it was discovered they were girls, Perky thought it was funny to encourage Greta to name them Princess Elizabeth and Princess Margaret Rose, like the real princesses at Windsor Castle.

"Oh, Perky, you are terrible!" cried Maisie Gills, who had come to look after Greta. "You can't name a piglet after a princess!" The poor young babysitter got such a terrible attack of the giggles that the cup of tea she was drinking went right up her nose. Her already pink cheeks turned scarlet and things were only made worse when Greta insisted on thumping her on the back – quite hard.

"Stop!" she squealed. "I don't care what you call the wretched piglets, just let me get a hankie and blow my nose."

Unfortunately for Perky, his suggestion was also overheard by the colonel, who had driven up early that morning to deliver the churns.

"Have some respect, lad," he barked. Poor Perky looked as if he wished a hole in the ground would open up and swallow him. "You cannot name piglets after members of the British Royal Family. That sort of thing's no good for morale."

"It was only a spot of fun," Perky mumbled.

"Silly boy," said Greta, shaking her head as if she would never have dreamed of naming a piglet after a princess, even though her eyes had lit up at the thought.

"Just remember, young man," said Colonel Crowther. "Princess Elizabeth will be our queen one day."

"Do you know them, Colonel? The princesses, I mean," said Edie, trying to draw attention away from poor Perky, whom she knew hadn't meant any real harm. The old colonel seemed so proud and proper, she wouldn't be at all surprised if he was personally acquainted with royalty.

"I did meet their Royal Highnesses on one occasion," he said. "When I was dining with the king."

"Oh," gasped Edie. "How exciting."

"Did they have their crowns on?" asked Greta.

"Of course." He chuckled. "That's how I knew they were proper princesses."

"Golly!" Greta squealed with excitement. "Were they sitting on thrones?" she asked. "Did they have unicorns?"

"I believe they did," teased the colonel.

But Aunt Roberta stepped in. "Come along, now. We mustn't hold the poor colonel up. He is a very busy man. Thank you so much for bringing the churns, Colonel Crowther."

"My pleasure," he said, almost bowing to Aunt Roberta as if she was a queen. "I think this pig club of yours was a wonderful idea, my dear lady. And don't you worry, I've got my eye on those Snigson brothers. They're both in the Home Guard, you know. I've put them on extra duties. That'll make sure they don't get up to too much mischief."

Uncle Peter came to the door and saluted as the colonel drove away.

"Didn't you ever want to be in the Home Guard too, Uncle Peter?" asked Gus as they watched the colonel's little black car rattle away down the hill.

Edie coughed and trod on his foot, hard! Couldn't he see it was a stupid question? It seemed obvious to her that Uncle Peter wouldn't want to have anything to do with guns and fighting any more, even if it was only practice in the fields and lanes.

"I'm not much use to them, I'm afraid. Not with this limp." Uncle Peter tapped his bad leg. But Edie wondered if it was more about the noise and bangs. She had noticed even when he was building a pigpen for the Twiglets that he shuddered every time he brought the hammer down on a nail.

"There are plenty of other ways to help the war effort without being in the Home Guard," said Aunt Roberta firmly. "Uncle Peter translates important documents for the government. . ."

"That's why I'm here, as it happens." Perky dug into his postbag. "Aunty Patsy thought you might want this delivered PDQ!"

"PDQ?" said Edie.

"Pretty damned quick!" said both the boys, rolling their eyes at her.

Perky passed a big brown envelope to Uncle Peter. "Anything for me?" said Edie hopefully. She had finally received a long, newsy letter from Fliss at the beginning of the week. It began in blue ink, right back on the very first night she'd arrived at the base, then switched to green pen halfway through with news of her flying trips – although lots of that part had been scrawled out with thick black lines by the censor. Finally, Fliss finished off in pencil sending love, and a big red lipstick kiss, of course. Edie had read it and reread it a hundred times already.

"Sorry. Nowt else today." Perky climbed back on to his bike. "See you at RCHQ later," he mouthed. Then he rode away.

Uncle Peter's thick brown envelope certainly

looked impressive. It was covered with government seals and stamps and the word SECRET was printed in big red letters along the top.

"Blimey!" said Gus.

"It's not that exciting, I'm afraid." Uncle Peter shrugged. "It's probably just a shopping list from some poor chap in Berlin, reminding himself to buy toothpaste. . ."

"You speak German?" said Gus. He looked shocked.

Uncle Peter nodded. "I taught myself after the last war."

"That's amazing," said Edie. But Gus took a big step back. He scowled as if Uncle Peter had said he was Hitler himself, and Greta gave a funny squeal. Surely they didn't think Uncle Peter was some sort of terrible monster, just because he spoke German. He wasn't a Nazi in disguise. He was just using his language skills to help the war effort.

Gus had gone white as a sheet. He turned his back on Uncle Peter completely as if he couldn't even bear to look at him. Greta, on the other hand, seemed suddenly excited. She ran forward and shook Uncle Peter by the sleeve.

"What is it, mein Liebling?" He smiled.

"You can talk real, real German?" said Greta. "Like. . ." But before she could say another word, Gus grabbed her arm.

"Quick," he shouted. "We'll miss the 9.15 if we don't hurry."

In an instant, Uncle Peter's German skills were forgotten. "See you later," cried Edie.

The three children sped away across the field. Gus was practically dragging Greta with him as they ran. He seemed to be hissing something in her ear. Probably another brother and sister row. Edie left them to it. She ran fastest of all, desperate to reach the train in time. They'd been so busy settling the Twiglets in and doing their other chores, it had been days and days since she had last sent her love to Fliss by the Green Dragon.

That afternoon, the three older children met at HQ whilst Greta stayed at home with Maisie, who had brought her knitting bag from the village and promised to help make Mr Churchill a scarf. Maisie had also baked a delicious bread pudding from a leftover loaf and allowed Gus and Edie to take a thick slice each away with them on their adventure, and one for Perky too.

When the cake had been eaten, and every precious sultana savoured, Edie and the boys agreed to take turns to sit at the far end of the old dining carriage with the binoculars trained on Boar's Head Farm.

Perky was on duty first. While he was on watch, Gus took a brown post office notebook out of his pocket. Perky had given them one each, just as he had promised. There had been a leak in the storeroom last winter and the covers were a bit water-damaged and some of the pages stuck together, but other than that they were as good as new.

"Make do and mend!" as Edie had said, gratefully echoing the familiar wartime motto, when she had been given hers.

Gus pulled a stubby pencil out from behind his ear. He was clearly excited about something. "We know for sure the Snigsons were responsible for smuggling the Twiglets into the village," he said. "And I've been keeping track of their activities ever since."

Edie glanced over his shoulder at the page. All she could see was a lot of squiggles. "What's all that gubbins?" she asked.

"It's not gubbins." Gus sounded very insulted. "It's code! If my notebook falls into enemy hands, all they'll see is a secret cypher. My father uses code all the time when he is on top-secret missions, you know."

"Ah!" said Edie, frowning at the funny mixture of symbols and letters: $NN \rightarrow 2p\ RS = X$.

"Don't you see? NN is Len Snigson," explained Gus. "I used the last letters of both his names. And the arrow means he collected something."

"2p?" Edie scratched her head.

"Two piglets," sighed Gus. "From the RS."

"Railway station!" cried Edie. At least that bit was simple. "But what does the cross mean...?"

"It means: Len *didn't* collect the two piglets because Greta took the pram away." Gus tapped his pencil on the page. "Do you see that now?"

"Sort of," said Edie, sending a cloud of dust into the air as she flopped down on one of the long seats by the window. All this code seemed to be an awful lot of fuss and bother for something they already knew.

"What about the conversation we overheard by the railway line when we saw the Dark Demon?" she asked. "Do you think that was about the piglets too?"

"I'm not sure," said Gus. It was his turn to look awkward now. "I hadn't actually come up with my code back them. So I didn't note it all down. Not word for word, I mean."

"I did," cried Edie waving her own little post-office book in the air.

"In code?" groaned Perky, peering at her over the top of the binoculars. He'd only used his book to make paper aeroplanes and to leave a note for Aunty Patsy saying he'd be back in time for tea.

"It's more like a story, actually. A chronicle of our adventures," said Edie grandly. She liked the way that sounded. It was becoming clear she wasn't really cut out to be a spy. She thought perhaps she'd rather write books when she grew up.

"*A hunched figure came out of the mist. . .*" she began.

"There wasn't any mist that morning," said Gus.

Edie ignored him. "*A hunched figure came out of the mist. . . It was Len Snigson.*"

"Len doesn't have a hunched back," said Perky.

"Do you want to hear what he said or not?" snapped Edie. But she could tell the boys weren't going to listen properly, so she skipped on to the part where Len actually spoke: "'*Listen, Donny, I'm telling you, it's somewhere here,' he told his brother. 'From this telegraph pole, all the way back to the mouth of the tunnel.' The railwayman's rasping voice was as clear as a snarling dog in the morning air...*" Edie was especially proud of that last line.

"Hmm," said Perky with a cheeky grin. "It isn't a patch on the tale of the Ghostly Signalman... I should tell you that sometime."

"But it is true. I'll give Edie that," said Gus. "The bit about what Len said, at least, once you've got rid of all the mist and snarling. The brothers were definitely interested in that stretch of track. They started pacing up and down, as if they were measuring it out."

"Perhaps they were looking for a message telling them which train to expect the piglets to arrive on?" said Edie.

"If someone was sending a message, surely they'd have agreed on an exact place to leave it," said Gus.

"Maybe it was written on a piece of paper and it blew away in the wind?" suggested Edie.

But Gus shook his head. "In that case, they'd have had no idea where to start. They were only looking along the edge of the track."

"True," sighed Edie. She had to admit Gus was good at this sort of thing.

"Come on," said Perky, springing up from his lookout post. "There's nowt happening on the farm. We should go and have a look by this famous telegraph pole. Perhaps you missed summat."

"All right," agreed Edie, although she wished they could stay in the dining carriage a bit longer. She had always wanted her very own secret camp – somewhere she could play make-believe. They didn't have a garden in Glasshouse Street, not even so much as a window box. The old railway carriage was even better than a real Wendy house would have been.

But the boys were already out the door, balancing on the fallen tree trunk, which acted like a drawbridge, and jumping down to the bank below. Edie followed and together they walked all the way back to the part of the line near the telegraph pole and paced up and down the edge of the railway, searching the same stretch of ground until their legs ached.

"It would help if we knew what we were looking for," grumbled Perky. But he was far too busy trying to frighten Gus and Edie with his terrible tale of the Ghostly Signalman to be much use anyway.

"He had his head sliced off by a train way back in 1866," he whispered, raising his hands like a spectre. "Whooo!"

"Oh, for goodness' sake!" Edie laughed. Perky was

just about the most friendly looking ghost she'd ever seen.

Even so, she couldn't help screaming when he leapt out at her from behind a bush five minutes later.

They gave up after that and trudged home, no closer to solving the mystery of what the Snigsons had been up to that day on the side of the tracks.

That night, as she lay in bed, Edie couldn't get thoughts of the horrible headless signalman out of her mind. Suddenly Perky's silly story and his ghostly moans didn't seem quite so funny any more.

I'll keep out of Perky's way for a few days until he's forgotten all about it, she decided sleepily. *It'll serve him right.*

But, the very next morning, Perky was back.

"Edie," he cried, dropping his bike and running across the meadow while she was milking Mr Hitler. "I've another telegram for you." He waved the thin brown envelope in the air.

Edie froze. She tried to remember what Perky had said last time: telegrams didn't always bring bad news.

She stood up, very slowly, clutching the milking pail.

She was trembling a little. She couldn't help it. It was as if the Ghostly Signalman himself had run an icy finger down her spine.

"Here!" She thrust the metal pail into Perky's hands. "You can finish milking Mr Hitler, can't you?" she said. Without waiting for his answer, she grabbed the telegram and ran.

If it was bad news, she wanted to be alone when she read it. She kept running until she reached the wooden fence above the railway line – the place where they waved to the 9.15.

She sat down on the sunny bank and ripped the envelope open with one quick tear, like pulling a sticking plaster off her knee. With trembling hands, she unfolded the paper and read:

B-U TOMORROW = FLISS

For a moment, Edie wasn't sure what to think. It wasn't bad news at least. Fliss had sent the telegram herself, which showed she was safe and well. But what did it mean?

"B-U tomorrow," Edie mumbled. "*Be you...?*" Why

did everything in this war have to be in code? Then suddenly, she leapt in the air and cheered, sending a pair of pheasants screeching into the sky.

"B-U!" she cried. "Of course! Beat-up." She remembered the daring low flights Belinda Barton-Withers had described. She'd said it was what the ATA pilots did when they got a chance to fly near home, or where their loved ones were, at least. No wonder Fliss had written in code, or the censor would have stopped her for sure.

Perhaps that was why Fliss had given no exact time for her flight, either. Edie worried for a moment that she might miss her altogether, but realized with a rush of relief that whatever time the plane came the next day she would be sure to hear it as soon as it flew near.

Her heart soared. Fliss was coming. She was going to do a beat-up. Right here above Three Chimneys. Tomorrow.

Chapter Thirteen

The Storm

Edie woke with a start to the sound of Uncle Peter shouting again – more like screaming this time than actual words. It was followed by Aunt Roberta's hurried footsteps rushing along the landing to his room.

She sat up in bed and hugged her knees as she listened to the murmuring voices down the hall.

It must be the middle of the night, she thought. She could hear the wind rattling the windows and Greta's steady sleeping breaths beside her. In the glow of the night light, she could see Greta's little blonde head resting on Mr Churchill, her fingers wound round the smart new stripy scarf that Maisie had knitted for him.

Greta could probably have slept through a direct hit in the Blitz! But Edie knew there was no point in trying to get back to sleep herself. It had taken her long enough to drop off in the first place. She was too excited about seeing Fliss fly low over Three Chimneys for her promised beat-up. It was only a few hours away now at the most. She swung her feet out of bed, pulled on a sweater and crept to the door.

It was so dark in the house with the blackout curtains drawn that she tripped over the rug at the top of the stairs and thumped down the first three steps on her bottom.

"Ow!" She tried to stifle a groan.

"Shh! Keep it down," hissed a voice in the darkness below. As Edie heaved herself to her feet, she could just make out the shadowy figure of Gus in the gloom of the kitchen.

She scrambled down the last few steps to join him. She didn't need to ask why he was awake too as another yell rang out from the floor above.

"Poor Uncle Peter," she whispered.

"Shall we get out of here?" suggested Gus. "We could go down to the railway."

"All right," she agreed, feeling her way towards the back door.

Perhaps they'd be in time to see the Dark Demon hurtling past again. But as they stepped on to the porch, Edie saw that they were probably too late. The first light of dawn was already tinting the sky, turning it from deep soot black to swirling grey. It was raining too, and the wind she'd heard at the blacked-out windows was stronger than she'd thought, whipping round the side of the house in a blustery summer squall.

She felt a sudden twist of panic – would Fliss still fly in this weather? She couldn't bear the thought of not seeing her. But, more than anything, she didn't want her taking risks.

"Should we go back?" Gus whispered, holding his palm out beyond the porch to feel the rain.

"No. Let's keep going." She stamped her feet into her wellington boots. "It's only drizzling really." It wasn't true, but she felt better as soon as she said it. The ATA wouldn't stop flying just because of a bit of rain, even if it was quite heavy. This was England.

They'd never get anything done if they were afraid of getting wet. "We could borrow those," she said, pointing to a couple of dusty old mackintoshes hanging in the porch.

"Good idea!" Gus took a long black one, which probably belonged to Uncle Peter. Hers was dark green or navy, she couldn't quite tell in the half-light, but it smelt of dust and wax and, very faintly, of Aunt Roberta – not Chanel perfume like Fliss, but dried lavender.

"Come on." They began to run towards the railway line, the wind buffeting against them. The coat was far too big for Edie, but she was glad of it, and she turned the collar up against the rain. She was pleased she had put her wellies on too. The grass in the meadow had grown long in the last few sunny weeks and it was soaking wet around the hem of her nightdress.

As soon as they were far enough away from the house not to see it behind them in the gloom, Edie slowed down. It was easier to walk than to run on the soggy ground, especially with the wind in her face.

After a few more paces, she stopped completely. The rain was pelting down now. She threw her head back and let it fall on her cheeks.

"Sure you don't want to go back?" said Gus.

"No point." Edie laughed. "We're soaking wet already!" She opened her mouth and tried to catch the raindrops. As she stood there, she thought she heard a sound. Not just the wind but a low, buzzing drone.

"Listen." She caught hold of Gus's arm. "Can you hear it?"

Gus cocked his head.

"I think it's a plane," he said, tilting his face towards the sky. He held his hand up to protect his eyes from the rain.

"Can you see anything?" asked Edie. All she could make out in the dim light were heavy clouds. The rain was driving down in spears. Even so, she felt a rush of excitement. Perhaps Fliss was flying over already. Belinda Barton-Withers had said the women delivering planes were often up at the crack of dawn.

She ran forward, stumbling towards the higher ground. "We'll get a better view up here," she called over her shoulder to Gus. She slipped on the soggy slope, her hands plunging into muddy soil. As she stood up, she saw a flash of bright light on the horizon and heard a great boom of thunder.

"It's a storm," cried Gus. And he opened and closed

his mouth as if he was trying to say something, but Edie couldn't hear his words. There was another crack of lightning and the air was filled with a great booming roar – not thunder this time, but the unmistakable whir of a plane's engine almost on top of them.

A dark shadow burst out of the clouds, and a huge bomber loomed above, like a giant iron bird.

"It's so low," cried Edie, as it spluttered over their heads. Was this Fliss, swooping down for her beat-up?

"Too low!" yelled Gus.

There was a blaze of orange light in the grey sky. Edie shielded her eyes, thinking for a moment that it was another flash of lightning streaking across the sky. Then she realized the light was coming from the plane. It was on fire.

"No!" cried Edie. She clutched her stomach.

"It's been hit," yelled Gus. "It's going to crash." There was a terrible booming sound and he pushed Edie to the ground.

She hurled him aside and staggered to her feet.

"Edie, don't. . ." Gus grabbed the hem of her coat and tried to pull her back, but she slipped her arms out of the mackintosh and wriggled free.

"Fliss," she screamed, running forward. The stricken plane was plunging down towards the thick trees in the wood on the other side of the railway.

There was a deafening bang and a huge ball of fire filled the sky. Great plumes of dark black smoke rose into the grey cloud.

"No. . ." Edie felt as if she was going to throw up. She sank down in the mud, clutching her stomach. She was soaked to the skin, her wet nightdress clinging to her.

"Edie." Gus rushed forward and wrapped the coat around her. "It's all right." He shook her gently by the shoulders. "Listen to me, Edie. . . It's not your mother. It can't be. That plane wasn't one of ours. It was German."

"German?" It took Edie a moment to understand what he was saying.

"It was a Junkers 88," Gus explained, in a shaky voice. "I recognized it from my aeroplane book."

"Oh!" Edie staggered to her feet, relief washing over her. It wasn't Fliss who had crashed. . . She slipped her arms back into the sleeves of the mackintosh and hugged herself tight.

"It was definitely a German Junkers," said Gus.

"Although the engine didn't sound right. There was clearly something wrong."

"Poor things," whispered Edie, thinking of the crew. The plane had gone up like a fireball. They must have died for sure. She knew they were Germans and she was supposed to hate them. But she couldn't. Not while she stared at the plumes of black smoke rising up from the wood. It could so easily have been Fliss.

"They're the enemy," snapped Gus. "They came here to drop bombs, remember."

"I know," said Edie. She was too tired and cold to argue. The storm had passed over, but it was still raining heavily.

"Go home and get dry," said Gus. "I'm going to the woods to see where it came down." His eyes were flashing with excitement. She should have guessed that the boy who spent half his life with his head in an aeroplane book would be desperate to see a real crashed plane – especially an enemy one.

"Wait!" said Edie. "I'm coming too."

Gus didn't argue. "If we cross the railway line over the bridge by the canal, we should be able to get into the woods from there," he said.

They were running now, squelching over the soft mud.

"Gus!" Edie gasped as the railway line came into view beneath them. "Look! There's something on the track."

It was an enormous lump of twisted grey metal as big as a boulder.

"It's from the plane!" Gus was already leaping over the fence and slithering down the bank beyond. "It's a propeller and part of one of the engines," he called as she followed him down. "It must have broken free before the crash."

"What should we do?" said Edie.

Gus was standing on the tracks, staring at the jagged wreckage.

"Help me!" She rammed her shoulder hard against the pile of twisted metal. But it was hopeless it didn't budge an inch. "Don't you see?" she cried. "It's blocking the track. If a train comes there's going to be a terrible smash."

Gus leapt forward and began heaving his weight against it too. But it was no good. They were like two ants trying to shift an elephant.

"Look." Edie pointed to where the iron railway line had twisted and buckled with the force of the crash. Even if by some miracle they could move the wreckage aside, any train coming this way would still be derailed as it thundered over the broken tracks.

"We'll have to go to the station and warn them," said Gus, glancing at his watch. "Come on!" He began to run down the line in the direction of the village. "Thank goodness the Dark Demon passed by long ago."

"Wait!" cried Edie. "What is the time, anyway?"

"About ten to six," he called over his shoulder.

"Stop!" she cried. It wasn't the Dark Demon with its cargo of weapons they had to worry about. She remembered the early morning train which had followed after it and the sleepy passengers they had seen with their heads resting against the windows. "You'll never make it to the station. Not before the Dreaming Dragon is due."

"The 6.06!" Gus spun around and started running back towards her. "You're right, there's no time. What should we do?"

"We're going to have to stop the train," said Edie.

"Stop it," said Gus. "How?"

"I don't know," said Edie desperately. "But Aunt Roberta, Uncle Peter and Fliss did it years ago when some trees fell on the line. Aunt Roberta waved her petticoats at the train driver and he stopped just in time." But her heart sank as she glanced down at what she was wearing – the dark mackintosh and her soaking-wet fawn-coloured nightdress. It was hopeless – and Gus was just as bad in his long black coat and blue pyjamas. Not a red flannel petticoat between them – nothing they could wave in front of the train to bring it to a halt.

"I reckon we've got about eleven minutes until the train reaches this part of the line." Gus held up his watch for her to see.

"Then we need to think quickly," said Edie. "We have to do something. If the train comes round that corner, it'll be going too fast to stop. It'll smash into the wreckage and come off the tracks. Everyone on board will be killed."

"Not everyone, I shouldn't think," said Gus.

"Oh, shut up," she screamed. Why was he always so exact? This was no time to be such a prig. Then she realized he was probably only trying to comfort her a little.

"Surely someone will come," she said. "I know it's still early, but somebody must have heard the plane crash."

"I'm not sure," said Gus. "What with the storm. And even if they do, they'll go into the woods where they can see the smoke. That's where the main fuselage will be."

"Hello!" hollered Edie. "Hello." But there was nothing. She was wasting time.

"Let's go round the corner," said Gus. "The more space we give the train to slow down, the better. We can try waving the mackintoshes. It the best hope we have."

"The only hope," said Edie. But it wasn't much. Why would a train stop just because two children were waving their coats on the edge of the line? The driver probably wouldn't even see them, not through the thick grey drizzle. He probably wouldn't even see a red petticoat in this weather, even if she had been wearing one.

But as Edie turned the corner she gasped in disbelief. "Look!" A bright white sheet was hanging from the thorn trees on the bank.

"It's as if it's been sent by an angel," she cried. White was about the only colour that would show up in this dreadful weather.

"It's only a bed sheet!" said Gus. "It must have been blown off someone's washing line in the storm." But as Edie reached up to pull it down from the thorns, she saw that it wasn't a sheet at all. The material was slippery in her fingers, like silk.

Gus stretched out his hand and felt it too. "It's a parachute," he said. "From the plane."

Edie's mind was whirring, but there was no time to think of anything but stopping the train.

"Have you got a knife?" she asked, tugging at the fabric with her teeth and trying to rip it.

"No," said Gus. "I'm wearing my pyjamas, remember."

"Try the coat," said Edie, stuffing her hands into the pockets of her mackintosh too. But there was nothing.

Gus shook his head. "Empty."

The parachute was huge. "We have to tear it into strips somehow," said Edie. "Or we won't be able to wave it." She tried desperately to rip it against a sharp thorn poking out of the tree, but it was no good. All she did was prick her fingers.

"I've got a better idea!" said Gus. He started pulling the parachute free from the trees and dragging it back along the line. "We can use the jagged metal on the wreckage," he panted. "We can cut it on that."

"There isn't time," said Edie, but she started

dragging the parachute too. There was nothing else for it.

Gus was right. As they snagged the fabric back and forward across the sharp edges of the wreck, it frayed and tore. Soon Edie was able to rip it into rough untidy squares. Although her fingers were shaking, it felt good to be doing something useful – just like getting ready for the air-raid warnings in London. At least they had a plan. It helped to still her panic just a bit.

"Run," she said, gathering bundles of white material in her arms. There were only minutes left but it was no good unless they were round the corner, on the long straight stretch where the train could see them and had time to stop. Gus sprinted off but, in her haste, Edie dropped half her pieces of fabric and turned back to pick them up. She crouched down, gathering them into her arms.

As she straightened up again, she screamed. A pale figure was standing over her in the drizzle.

For a moment she thought it was Perky's ghostly signalman – except this figure still had his head. He was wearing a flying helmet and a boiler suit.

"*Schnell*," he said. "*Schnell, bitte!*"

"German," gasped Edie. "Of course." He was from

197

the plane. He must have used the parachute to bail out before the crash. She wanted to run, but all she could do was stand frozen on the spot as the airman stretched out his hands towards her. She flinched, sure that he was going to hurt her. But he tried to grab the squares of material from her instead.

"Thief!" cried Edie. "Get off." She stamped on his toes, her arms flailing wildly with panic. Perhaps he wanted to surrender, and needed to wave a white flag. But he couldn't take the strips of material from her. Not now. She needed them to stop the train. She struggled and pulled against him like a tug of war.

After only a second or two the airman let go and scrambled up the bank above her.

"Gus!" she yelled. "Help." Gus came running back along the track.

"He's German," cried Edie, pointing to the airman. "What do we do? He's getting away." She was sure they ought to try and take him prisoner, but there was no time.

"We have to save the train," said Gus desperately. "There's less than five minutes."

He was right. She thought she could hear a distant rumble chugging towards them already.

She glanced up at the bank. "Oh, no!" The airman

wasn't running away at all. He had pulled a young tree up by the roots and he was swinging it above his head like a cudgel. "He's going to attack us," she cried.

"*Nimm den*," he bellowed. "*Eine Flagge!*"

Gus scrambled up the bank and grabbed a stick of his own.

"Don't!" screamed Edie. "For goodness' sake, Gus. Don't fight him. He'll kill you."

But the airman didn't hit Gus with the young tree. Instead, he threw it down the bank and began pulling others from the ground.

"Flagpoles!" shouted Gus and at last Edie understood.

Gus tossed her a long thin stick and she tied two corners of one of the ragged squares of parachute to it, then she dug it into the wet ground like a flag at the side of the tracks.

Gus did the same. All the while, the German airman was helping them.

At last, there was a line of wobbly flags along both sides of track. Edie and Gus still had one each. The airman took a flag too.

Edie smiled at him, wishing she had the words to thank him for everything he had done.

"Ready?" Gus leapt across to the far side of the track.

"Ready!" Edie's voice was barely more than a croak. She raised her flag. The chug of the train was louder now and she could see the smoke above the trees. She felt sick to her stomach. They had just one chance to stop it, or the train would smash into the wreckage on the line taking all its carriages with it and people would be killed for sure.

"*Ja*. Rea-dy!" said the German. And he smiled back at Edie. He had taken his flying helmet off and she could see that he was young. His blond hair was stuck to his head and streaked with rain.

"Thank you," she whispered.

And, next moment, the train thundered into view like a great dragon billowing smoke.

"Stop!" Edie began to wave her flag and yell. "Stop!" she cried, leaping up and down. "Stop the train!"

Chapter Fourteen

"Our Duty In A Time Of War"

The train kept coming, roaring along the line towards them.

"Stop!" cried Edie. Her ears were pounding and her nose and throat were full of the sooty smell of smoke. "Stop! Oh, please stop!" Her voice was drowned out by the rattle and roar of the engine. She leant forward, right over the edge of the tracks, and waved her flag frantically in the air. Out of the corner of her eye, she saw the German airman waving too.

"It's no good," she cried, and without even thinking, she grabbed his arm. "It's no good at all." If the train crashed, hundreds of people might be killed, it was travelling so fast. Pictures flashed through her mind of all the awful things she'd seen in London – bombed buildings, injured people, the broken shell of the Café de Paris. She couldn't bear for something terrible to happen here too – not when she'd felt so safe at Three Chimneys. She had to stop that train!

Edie sprang forward, leaping over the wet rails and stood in the middle of the track itself, waving her flag more frantically than ever.

"*Vorsicht!*" cried the German, panic rising in his voice.

"Get back!" roared Gus from the other side. Edie knew she should listen. She knew it was dangerous and stupid to stand on the line, especially with the train hurtling towards her. But she had to make it stop.

Through the thick drizzle she heard a scream of breaks and a hiss of steam.

"It's working," she cried. "See!"

The train seemed to be slowing down at last.

She waved her flag one more time and leapt towards the safety of the bank. But her foot slipped on the wet rail as she jumped.

She heard her own voice scream – as if it was someone else very far away – and everything seemed to go into slow motion as she fell. Sharp pain seared through her knee as she hit the track. She tried to scramble to her feet, but her legs were caught up in the hem of the long mackintosh and she struggled like a fly in a web. She looked up and saw the train looming down on her – a roaring, rattling mass of flying sparks and flashing metal.

"Help!" she screamed. And she felt a hand grab her collar. She was whirled through the air so fast, everything was a blur.

Next thing she knew, she was lying on the wet grass and the German airman was staring down at her. The train had finally screeched to a halt. It was juddering and shuddering on the rails, shivering like an angry iron stallion, just a few inches from where she lay.

"We did it!" she murmured. The train had been stopped – they had prevented the crash. She closed her eyes for a moment and took a long, deep breath.

By some miracle, she was still alive. All because the German airman had pulled her from the tracks.

"Thank you," she whispered. "You saved my life."

But, as she lifted her head, she saw that the young man had gone. He had vanished, melting away into the smoke and rain.

Edie was still trembling as the driver jumped down from the train. She had a big gash on her knee and stood, leaning on Gus's shoulder.

"What the blazes did you kids think you were doing?" roared the engine driver. "It's an offence to stop a train . . . not to mention how you could have been killed!"

"But . . ." said Edie weakly. She really couldn't find the words to explain. "There's a plane . . ." She waved her hand up the line in the direction of the wreckage.

"A what?" snapped the driver. Passengers were leaning out of the carriages now, staring down the line.

"A plane," said Gus. "Or part of one, at least."

"He's right," cried the sooty-faced fireman, who had jumped down, still holding his shovel from heaving coal into the engine, and run to the bend in the track. "I can see it. It's blocking the whole bleeding line too. We'd have all been goners if we'd hit that!"

Word seemed to travel fast then, and all the passengers leaning out of the window began to clap and cheer. "These kids saved the train!" she heard a sailor in a white hat shout. Edie steadied herself against Gus's shoulder. She tried to smile, but still felt a little sick.

"I owe you an apology," said the driver, when he had been to look at the wreckage for himself. "You youngsters saved a lot of lives today, and no mistake." He shook them both by the hand. "Without your quick thinking, there would have been a terrible catastrophe."

Gus cleared his throat. "Thank you, but we were only doing our duty in a time of war," he said in a stiff little voice.

"Oh, dear!" A laugh escaped from Edie's lips. She couldn't help it. Maybe it was the shock or the throbbing in her ears or the pain in her knee, but it suddenly seemed terribly funny that Gus was trying to be so serious and sounding so grown up.

The engine driver looked at her as he wiped his brow with his sleeve. "You all right there, Miss?"

"Never better," said Edie. But that only made

her laugh even more. Then suddenly she wasn't laughing, she was crying and her nose was running and she was biting her lip.

"Sorry!" she said to Gus. She knew how he hated a fuss, but she saw that his eyes were shiny with tears too.

"Better get you home, I think," said the driver, and he motioned towards the engine. All the passengers began to clap and cheer again as Gus and Edie turned around.

Edie swallowed hard.

"Thank you!" she said. "Thank you very much."

Gus was blinking a little and mumbling something else about honour and duty. This time she didn't laugh. Instead she gave his shoulder a quick squeeze. They had done it. They had saved the train, all by themselves ... except it wasn't by themselves, of course. The German airman had been there too.

Edie felt her stomach tighten with anxiety. She glanced along the edge of the tracks, searching for any sign of him. She saw Gus looking too, his eyes scanning the trees on the bank. But neither of them said a word.

She knew they should raise the alarm. There was an enemy airman loose in the countryside. He was

German, and everyone said the Germans were bad. But he had saved her life. He had saved hundreds of lives. He could have hidden in the bushes or fled, leaving them to stop the train alone. But he had stayed to help them. He might be the enemy, but he was a good man too, she was sure of that.

Her head was spinning, but in spite of the twisting worry in her stomach, she saw that it had turned into a beautiful day. It had stopped raining at last and pale morning sun was breaking through the clouds, making everything sparkle where it was still wet.

"Hop up quick," said the driver and before Edie could say another word, he helped her scramble into the cab of the train. The step was so high she wouldn't have been able to climb in by herself even if she didn't have a sore knee. The driver gave Gus a bunk-up too and he squeezed in beside her on a little metal seat, next to the pit of roaring coals that drove the engine.

"I'll need to propel the train backwards to the station and warn them," shouted the driver above all the noise and clatter of the cab. "It's not an easy business – especially with all these carriages. But the sooner we get back there, the sooner they can telegraph for help."

He was already turning nobs and twisting dials, which hissed steam as the fireman shovelled coals.

Gus's eyes were wide as he stared at all the levers and pistons.

"What's that one for?" he asked, leaping to his feet as soon as the train was chugging backwards.

"That's the injector," hollered the driver. "It fills up the boiler, see? And this here's the automatic brake. . ."

While they were all looking at the engine and leaning out of the windows to stare down the line, Edie rolled up the edge of her sodden nightdress to examine her knee.

It wasn't too bad, really. Just a deep cut. She'd had worse when she'd skidded in the playground on ice, in the terrible cold winter they'd had this year. Being as clumsy as she was, Edie was never without a scab or a bruise somewhere on her legs and knees.

She realized she was still holding a strip of white parachute silk. Nobody had asked them how they had made the flags – not yet, at least, although there were bound to be questions later. She tied the material tight around her leg like a bandage. It would stop any bleeding. Then she pulled her nightie back down over her knee.

A moment later, the train screeched backwards into the station. Everybody began to shout and there was a great commotion up and down the platform as news passed back and forward.

The driver leapt down and helped Edie and Gus from the cab. Within minutes signals had been changed and emergency calls sent out so that every train coming from north and south and stations all along the line had been warned that the track was not safe.

Perky was on the platform too, almost dancing with excitement at all the drama. "Drawn to disaster like a wasp to jam," as his roly-poly aunty Patsy said, tweaking him by the ear.

"They've found the rest of the plane," said Perky, when he had finished congratulating them and slapping them both on the back. "Smashed to smithereens in Bailey's Wood. Aunty's got the pony and trap outside; she'll take us down to see it, if you like?"

"Oh!" Edie was still in a daze. She wasn't sure she wanted to go anywhere near the crash site just yet. Seeing the plane plunge into the trees from a distance had shaken her up badly enough. The thought of being up close to the wreckage made her shiver. Gus seemed to hesitate for a moment now too.

"Perhaps I should take you home instead? You must have had a terrible shock," said the post-mistress kindly.

"Erm. . ." Edie faltered for a moment, but Perky was already bustling them along the platform.

"Come on! How often do you get the chance to see a thing like this?" he said. "They reckon the plane might've been hit by an 'ack-ack' anti-aircraft gun in Maidbridge and tried to limp back to the coast. But then they got lost in the storm." He beamed at Gus and Edie. "Who says all the excitement's down in London, eh?"

"In you pop, then, if you're sure you're all right," said his aunty Patsy. She seemed excited to see the crash too. A chubby grey pony, as round and roly-poly as she was herself, was standing between the shafts of a cart outside. "I hope you don't mind a bit of squeeze." She pointed to a sack full of letters and parcels. "I've got all my deliveries over Marlow Bridge way to do, yet."

And before Edie knew it, they were on their way.

News travelled fast and most of the village seemed to have come to the wood to see the German plane.

Chunks of twisted wreckage were strewn between

the trees. People scrambled amongst the debris, chattering and calling out to one another: "There's a wheel here!" or "Look at this! I've found a piece of wing." It reminded Edie of holidaymakers rock-pooling at the beach. Some people had even brought picnic breakfasts and flasks of tea.

Edie wrapped the mackintosh tightly around her, so that nobody could see she was still in her nightdress underneath. Any time someone spotted her or Gus, they shook them warmly by the hand.

"We're all very proud of you for saving the train like that," said Reverend Greaves.

"That we are," agreed Mr Hodges, the butcher. "Mind and send your aunt to see me. Reckon I might have a nice bit of steak tucked away. Dinner for heroes, is steak."

"Thank you," said Edie. But she didn't feel like a hero. Not any more. All she could think about was the airman. Surely they ought to have told someone about him straight away. By now, he could be halfway to Maidbridge. He could have slipped away on to the moors where nobody could ever track him down. Worse still, he could be making plans to blow up a railway bridge. . . But if he was going to do that, why would he have helped them save the train?

Her head was pounding and her stomach felt worse. She knew the longer they left it to raise the alarm, the more trouble there would be in the end. Yet all she could think about was how brave and kind the airman had been.

Beside her, Gus looked pale and sick. He was biting his lip.

"What are we going to do?" she whispered. "We ought to say something."

"Shut up, can't you?" Gus hissed. They were only standing a few feet away from Captain Crowther who had gathered together some of the Home Guard. Len Snigson was leaning against a tree, smoking the stubby end of a cigarette.

"Listen up, men," the colonel boomed. "It appears a number of bodies have been found amongst the wreckage." He nodded his head towards the burnt-out shell of the cockpit in a clearing on the other side of the trees.

Edie could see Reverend Greaves with his head bowed saying a prayer.

"Serves them right! Sizzled like German sausage." Len Snigson laughed, taking a long draw on his cigarette.

Edie shuddered again. What a horrible man he was.

"Put that thing out and stand up properly. You're on duty now," barked Colonel Crowther.

Len sighed and rolled his eyeballs, but he did as he was told.

"At least one of the blighters must have escaped," said Mr Hodges. "Billy down on his barge reckons he saw a parachute floating in the canal."

"And there's bits of white silk on the edge of the railway too," panted Donny Snigson, skidding to a stop and saluting the colonel. He was bright red in the face and looked as though he might have run the whole way down the tracks from Boar's Head Farm so as not to miss the excitement.

Edie's tummy turned cartwheels.

The colonel bore down on her and Gus. "Parachute, eh?" he said. "Is that what you used to stop the train?"

"Yes," said Edie and Gus at the same time.

"We found it caught in the thorn trees," said Gus.

"We cut it into strips," explained Edie. They were gabbling so fast they were talking over each other.

"Hmm," said the colonel. Edie felt a huge sense of relief. She was almost dizzy. She knew what was coming next. He would ask them if they had seen anyone. This was their chance to explain about the airman and how

213

they hadn't had time to mention it sooner, what with all the shock and drama of saving the train.

But the colonel didn't ask them any more questions at all. "Good, good," he said, and shook their hands as if he was working the pump in his garden. "Well done again, youngsters. Quick thinking." Then he turned away and began to organize his men. "We need to be calm and thorough."

It was Len Snigson who spoke next. "If I find any Jerry airmen, I'll skin 'em alive," he said. "Then I'll hang 'em by their necks from the railway bridge."

From the way he narrowed his eyes, Edie had no doubt it was true.

"Don't suppose you saw anyone?" He spun round and stared at Edie and Gus.

Edie knew this was the moment that she ought to tell the truth. But all she could see were Len Snigson's little sharp teeth as he snarled like a terrier about to catch a rat. Her German . . . she had begun to think of him like that . . . *her* German had saved her life. And if Len Snigson found him, he would skin him alive.

"No," she said quietly. "We didn't see anyone."

"Not a soul," said Gus.

And that was it. The lie was told.

Chapter Fifteen

A Bad Day

Edie's head felt hot and fuggy. Her feet were freezing cold.

The last thing she remembered was coming back to Three Chimneys in the little post cart and Aunt Roberta and Uncle Peter congratulating them for saving the train.

"Not that I approve of you playing around on the railway tracks or being out and about at the crack of dawn," said Aunt Roberta sternly. But she handed them both a steaming mug of cocoa, and, for a moment, her hand rested gently on the top of Edie's head. "Thank goodness you're safe. Oh, thank goodness," she sighed.

Edie looked up at her and managed to smile.

She felt Aunt Roberta's love settling on her like a warm blanket. *How could I ever have thought she didn't care for me?* wondered Edie. But she couldn't drink the cocoa, even though there was probably a full week's ration of sugar in it. She couldn't even lift the mug. Her hands were shaking too much and her arms seemed like lead.

"Bed for you, young lady," ordered Aunt Roberta. "You've caught a chill. Not to mention all the excitement."

"Excitement?" said Edie, clinging to Aunt Roberta's arm. "It wasn't exciting, it was terrible."

Her head sank into her soft white pillow. She couldn't even remember coming upstairs, although she was wearing a clean, dry nightie. . .

"Goodnight," she whispered, lifting her head. But everybody seemed to have left already. Someone had pulled the blackout curtains and the night light was glowing.

Edie closed her eyes, but as soon as she did she

saw an image of the burning plane spiralling towards the ground.

"Wait!" she shouted – or at least she thought she did – but nobody came. "I need to get up."

Edie remembered that Fliss was coming. For the beat-up. She was going to fly over Three Chimneys.

She tried to swing her legs out of bed, but she couldn't. "Fliss?" she mumbled. But the shadow that came to the door was Aunt Roberta.

"Shh!" she whispered, and she pressed a cool flannel against Edie's burning forehead. "Try to get some sleep."

... The Twiglets were flying a Spitfire. It was low. Too low. Then suddenly it wasn't the Twiglets at all. It was the German, her German... He was waving a white flag.

Edie tossed and turned in her sleep as images of roaring trains and burning planes filled her dreams. Len Snigson yapped like a terrier and Colonel Crowther, for no reason at all, had turned into an old grey wolf.

Then it was morning. Or, Edie guessed it must be. The blackout curtains were open a crack as if someone had lifted them and peeped out. A beam of sunlight danced across the floor.

Edie stretched.

"About time!" said a small, impatient-sounding voice.

Edie pulled herself up and saw Greta standing over her with her arms crossed.

"Hello." She blinked. "Have I been asleep long?"

"Very long," said Greta. She uncrossed her arms and began to count on her chubby little fingers. "One, two, three whole days."

"Three days?" Edie's throat felt dry and sandy, but the stiffness in her body was gone and her head wasn't burning any more. Suddenly she was wide awake. "I can't have been asleep for all that time," she gasped. "I need to see Fliss. Did she come?"

Greta padded over to the little fireplace that was never lit. She picked up a thin blue envelope which was propped up on the mantelpiece and padded back again. "This came for you."

Edie recognized Fliss's curly writing at once. She turned the envelope over and tore it open. There was a big red kiss on the back. Inside was a single sheet of writing paper:

Darling E

So sorry I could not come. All plans changed and rota shifted.

Rather beastly here, actually. Poor BBW had a terrible prang. She was killed, flying into a cliff near . . .

The name of the place had been blacked out and Edie couldn't read it. But she'd understood enough. BBW was Belinda Barton-Withers – and she had died flying a plane. Edie remembered how loud and jolly the young ATA pilot had been – so full of life, like the older girls at school when they were setting off for a hockey match. Edie had to catch her breath before she could look back at Fliss's letter.

The funeral is tomorrow. I know I shall weep buckets.

So sorry to miss you again. I love you, my darling

More soon.

F xoxo

P.S: Love to Pete and Roberta (I hope she isn't being TOO strict!)

P.P.S: Sorry so glum. Will send more news next

time. And maybe even a birthday visit if I can get leave – but promise not to hold your breath, sweetheart.

xoxo

Edie folded the letter into a tiny, tight little square, no bigger than a postage stamp. The sad note had made her feel so helpless. She was cross and miserable and tired. She wanted to scream and punch the wall.

"This bloody war! I *hate* it," she said. "This bloody, bloody war!"

She had been so wrapped up in her letter, she had forgotten Greta was there. The little girl gasped and her mouth fell open in surprise.

"You said a bad word!"

"I know," said Edie quickly. "I didn't mean it. I'm just . . . tired." She couldn't explain how she really felt. Sort of hollow inside – and not just because she hadn't eaten anything, but because of poor Belinda Barton-Withers and Fliss not coming and the plane crash too.

"Tired?" Greta snorted. "You can't be tired. You've already slept for. . ." She was holding up her fingers again and starting to count.

"Three days!" said Edie. "I know!" And she smiled. It was impossible to stay sad or cross for long with Greta around. "You don't know what the date is, do you?" She'd been asleep for so long, she couldn't quite work it out. Her birthday was on the twenty-third of the month; it must be only a few days now.

"Tuesday," said Greta. "No ... Wednesday, I think."

"Not the *day*," laughed Edie. "The *date*."

"It's the twentieth." Gus appeared in the doorway, clutching a tray with toast and tea. "I thought I heard your voice. Are you feeling better?"

"Much better," said Edie. But all thoughts of any birthday celebrations went out of her head the moment she saw Gus. All she could think about was the young German, and how they had let an enemy airman escape.

"Have they found him?" she whispered as Gus handed her the tray and perched on the edge of the bed.

"Found who?" said Greta.

"No one," said Gus and Edie, quickly. And as Edie took a sip of the hot sweet tea, Gus bustled Greta out of the door.

"I think the Twiglets are hungry," he said. "Colonel

Crowther just delivered a whole new churn of scraps. You ought to go down and see if Uncle Peter needs help feeding them."

"I want to stay with Edie," Greta whined.

"I've got my breakfast to eat. Those poor Twiglets must be starving," said Edie, through a mouthful of hot toast and sweet blackberry jam. It really was delicious after having an empty tummy for so long, even though there wasn't any butter, of course. You couldn't have butter *and* jam – not with the war on. Not even in the country.

"All right!" Greta hurried to the door. "I'll go and feed my Twiglets, but I'm coming right back."

"Good idea. I can't wait to hear what you've been up to," said Edie. "Send the Twiglets my love. . ."

They listened as she scampered away down the stairs.

Gus pushed the door closed with his foot.

"Go on, tell me," said Edie, cradling her warm mug of tea.

"There are four crew on a Junkers plane," Gus began to explain. "A pilot, an observer, a wireless operator and a gunner."

"Yes. But what about our one?" said Edie impatiently. "What happened to him?"

"I think they must've caught him," said Gus. "I heard Colonel Crowther telling Uncle Peter just now. He said there were at least two bodies in the wreckage and a Home Guard unit a couple of miles the other side of Stacklepoole found a German airman trying to steal a pail of milk from a dairy. And there's talk of another stowing away on a train as far as Leeds, but there've been so many rumours the last few days, it's been hard to keep up."

"And what'll they do with them now they've caught them?" said Edie, remembering Len Snigson's terrible boast to skin any enemy airmen alive.

"Colonel Crowther says they'll be sent to a prisoner-of-war camp," Gus explained. "They won't be harmed. The Germans do the same with captured British airman. Both sides will release them all at the end of the war."

"Well, that's not so bad," said Edie. At least their young airman would be safe now. Thank goodness fair-minded men like Colonel Crowther were in charge of the Home Guard, not bullies like Donny and Len Snigson.

"Easy for you to say!" Gus kicked at the skirting board. "You're not the one penned in behind barbed wire, living in a chicken hutch for the next ten years..."

"Ten years?" said Edie. "I'm sure the war won't go on that long."

But Gus seemed suddenly furious. He snatched the tray with her empty breakfast things. "I better get these washed up. Aunt Roberta's gone to work and Maisie's off with the flu." He stomped away down the stairs.

"Wait! What's wrong?" Edie called after him, but there was no reply. She lay back on her pillow and sighed. She couldn't work out what he was upset about at all. He was so odd and moody sometimes. He ought to be pleased. If their airman had been safely captured – and it sounded as if he had – then at least the terrible unpatriotic lie they had told about not seeing him didn't matter so much any more. No harm had been done.

Edie spent the rest of the morning sitting up in bed, cutting strings of paper dolls from an old newspaper with Greta. At lunchtime, Aunt Roberta came home to check on her.

She brought her a bowl of strong beef tea made with a piece of meat donated by the butcher. Not quite the steak he had promised, but good enough to boil. "It will build your strength up," said Aunt Roberta. "And

no running around for another day or two either."
Then she sat on the end of the bed and told Edie how
she used to love to play at being nurse when she was a
little girl. "Mother got sick when we first came to Three
Chimneys and the doctor always encouraged beef tea."

"Do you think that's why you decided to be a real
nurse when you grew up?" asked Edie.

"I do like feeling useful," said Aunt Roberta. "I
knew I wanted to train properly as soon as the Great
War came along. All the boys I knew, like Peter – and
our friend Jim – were going off to fight. I wanted to
be able to do something too. To help them when they
were injured. One heard such terrible stories."

"Weren't you very afraid?" asked Edie. She too had
heard terrible stories about that war and knew the
nurses had to work close to the fierce fighting in the
trenches.

"I was terrified," said Aunt Roberta truthfully.
"We were often up to our knees in thick mud with
no electric light and very little medicine to help the
wounded men. But it was better to be afraid and
doing something than just to be afraid. Think about
what you did when you saved the train. I am sure
you were frightened."

"I was," agreed Edie. When she closed her eyes,

she could still see the roaring train, thundering towards her. She could almost smell the smoke.

"And yet," said Aunt Roberta, "it would have been far worse just to stand and watch."

Edie nodded. It was true. "I think that's how Fliss feels about flying," she said. "She knows her job is dangerous. But she has to do her bit."

"Hmm." Aunt Roberta stood up. "I suppose so," she said. But her mood had changed instantly, as if a switch had been flicked.

"And she drove an ambulance in the last war," said Edie, suddenly feeling like she had to leap to Fliss's defence.

"That was different," said Aunt Roberta. "You weren't born then. She should have thought about that."

"What do you mean?" said Edie. Her chest felt tight. It had been so long since she had seen that look of disapproval on Aunt Roberta's face – but her forehead was deeply creased and the frown between her eyebrows was back.

"A baby is a very big responsibility," she sighed. "Fliss was on her own. All I'm saying is that she ought to have thought about that before she. . ."

"No!" Edie cut her off. "I don't want to talk about this any more," she said. "I'm tired."

She knew what Aunt Roberta was going to say and she couldn't bear to hear it. She was going to say Fliss should have thought before she had a baby on her own. Edie turned her face to the wall. She'd felt as if she'd grown so close to Aunt Roberta since she had come here, but all that made no difference in the end – Aunt Roberta still thought it would have been better if she hadn't been born at all.

"Edie?" Aunt Roberta touched her shoulder. "What's wrong?" But Edie shrugged her off.

"I'm tired," she whispered again, and she lay still under the hot heavy blankets until she heard Aunt Roberta leave the room.

As soon as she was gone, Edie threw back the covers. She got out of bed and flung open the window. She breathed in great gulps of fresh air. It had been a bad day. First Gus had got upset, although she still couldn't understand why. And now this with Aunt Roberta – was that how she really felt? That Fliss should never have had a baby at all?

"I don't care," said Edie, flopping back on to the bed. "I don't care what anyone thinks."

But she wished more than ever that she could see Fliss and be wrapped in a tight hug by her mother.

Chapter Sixteen

A Happy Birthday

By the next day, Edie felt a little better. The last of her aches and pains had gone and her spirits had lifted too. Neither she nor Aunt Roberta mentioned their conversation again.

"Just take one day at a time, and don't overdo things," Aunt Roberta said, kissing her warmly before she went to work.

"Yes, nurse!" Edie frowned thoughtfully, wondering if she'd got it all wrong. How could someone so kind and caring disapprove of something so much that they would fall out with their own sister?

"And not too much rich food for a while, either," said Aunt Roberta, climbing on to her bicycle.

Edie was soon allowed out and about again though, and by the time the morning of her birthday came around, she had almost forgotten she had been poorly at all.

She remembered how Fliss had begged her not to get her hopes up for a visit this time, so she decided that is exactly what she would do.

"If I don't have high hopes, they can't be dashed," she explained to Perky, who had come up early that morning to deliver the post to Three Chimneys.

Edie was sure she had seen more than one letter in his hand when he came through the door, but when she looked down at the kitchen table, there was only one of Uncle Peter's big brown envelopes with MOST SECRET written across the top.

She took a deep breath and battled with herself not to be disappointed – although she had been sure Fliss would have sent a card at least. It seemed everyone had forgotten it was her birthday. Uncle Peter was out in the vegetable patch, and Aunt Roberta was clattering around in the larder. Even Greta seemed to be busy with something outside, and Gus was making a pan of boiled eggs on the range.

Secretly, Edie had hoped there might be some sort of special birthday breakfast. It wasn't that she wanted a big fuss... Again she tried to fight down the rising feeling of disappointment. It was bound to be tricky to do anything much with the war on. Everyone was so busy and everything was in such short supply. Although they could grow their own food here, rations had to be shared fairly with people in the cities and towns.

Even so, she couldn't help thinking of the glorious birthday feasts she and Fliss used to have before the war broke out. They always went to Patisserie Valerie in Soho, a little cafe just around the corner from the flat. Fliss ordered coffee and Edie strawberry-flavoured milk and they both devoured huge slices of gooey Belgian chocolate cake with cream. This morning it looked as if she would have to make do with a boiled egg.

"Come on. Let's go for a walk," cried Perky, pulling her chair away as she tried to sit down.

"Now?" asked Edie in surprise. It looked as if she wasn't going to get any breakfast at all. He was practically dragging her to the door.

"Good idea," said Gus. "I'd come too, but I've got a Latin paper to do."

"Really?" Edie was amazed. Neither she nor Gus had been given any homework for ages. They'd barely even had a lesson for weeks – Aunt Roberta was busier than ever at the hospital and Uncle Peter was out digging in the garden from dawn to dusk, making the most of the good weather.

"It's time to start pulling my socks up and working hard, if I'm going back to school in September," said Gus.

"Fine." Edie gave in with a sigh. If that's how he felt, she'd leave him to it. She might as well go for a walk with Perky after all. "Save me a hard-boiled egg for later. I'll eat it cold," she said. Some birthday this had turned out to be.

Even Greta didn't bother to say good morning. Edie saw her scuttling away with a little basket behind the hen house as they ran off across the meadow.

"Shall we go and have a gander at where they're mending the line after the plane crash?" asked Perky.

"All right," agreed Edie. She had thought she wouldn't ever want to go anywhere near the place where they'd had to save the train, but she found she was curious to see it.

As they came to the top of the bank and looked down, she saw a large group of men working with shovels and picks on the rails. They were singing a loud, throaty song as they mended the line.

"Italians!" said Perky knowledgeably.

"Italians?" echoed Edie. Under Mussolini's rule, they were Britain's enemies, fighting alongside Hitler. "What are they doing here in Yorkshire?"

"Prisoners of war," said Perky. "Didn't you know? There's a big POW camp on the old racecourse outside Maidbridge. The government gets them to do work like this while our men are away fighting."

Edie watched as the prisoners shifted earth with their shovels and shored up the tracks. They were still singing with all their hearts and laughing too, even though Edie now noticed there was a guard with a rifle overseeing them. He was smiling and nodding his head as the Italians sang.

"There's no trains coming back through yet. They've had to divert them all to Maidbridge," explained Perky. "They'll have the whole lot shipshape again by tomorrow morning, first thing." There was no sign of the wreckage from the plane and new track had been laid too. "You've got to have the railways running in wartime, see."

"I suppose so," agreed Edie, remembering the Dark Demon speeding through the night with its cargo of weapons. The station was always busy with farmers too, loading essential supplies of food on to the trains so that people as far away as London, Liverpool or Leeds could have bacon, eggs, fresh milk and veg.

"Hitler would love to bring the railways to a standstill," said Perky. "Without trains the whole bloomin' country would grind to a halt."

Edie giggled. She knew he was making a serious point but he was starting to sound like the old men from the village who sat smoking their pipes and drinking pints of beer on the towpath outside the Rose and Crown. They were always predicting what would "bring the whole bloomin' country to a halt".

"If you're going to be like that, I reckon we can go home," said Perky.

"I'm sorry. I wasn't laughing at you. Not really," said Edie.

But Perky was already charging back up the meadow. "Come on! They should be ready for you by now."

"Ready for what?" shouted Edie. But Perky had bolted like a hare.

By the time Edie reached Three Chimneys, it was clear that something was afoot. She couldn't help smiling as Greta was poking her nose out of the kitchen door and giggling.

"Go away," she said. "We don't want you yet."

"Reckon I brought you back a little early," said Perky, looking sheepish and ducking inside.

"Go for a walk in the garden or something," said Gus, and the kitchen door was shut firmly in Edie's face.

As she wandered around the back of the house, she had a very odd feeling – a little out of sorts, yet excited all at the same time. She knew now, without a doubt, that whatever they were up to was for her benefit. But she still couldn't help feeling a little lonely and left out. She was just thinking how nice it would be to be allowed to help with the preparations for her own birthday, when Uncle Peter waved to her from his workshop in the stable yard.

"Poor Edie, are you an outcast?" he asked, pulling up a stool for her beside his tool bench.

"I'm afraid so." She smiled and felt better already. She loved coming into the stable workshop with its smell of copper polish and old leather. It was like an Aladdin's cave of long-forgotten treasure from the railways. The gentle tick of mended station clocks hummed in the air. In the corner beneath the hayrack where the horses used to eat, a pot-bellied stove from a platform waiting room was lying with its clawed feet in the air like a sleepy dragon.

Edie wondered if Uncle Peter knew about the abandoned dining car on the siding by the tunnel. She would have loved to tell him about it so he could restore it to its former glory – perhaps they could work on it together. But she knew the boys would never forgive her if she gave away the location of their HQ.

Instead, she picked up a pretty railway lantern that was sitting in the middle of the bench. It was about the size of the battered old kettle they boiled on the kitchen range to make tea, but it was much shinier. The brightly burnished copper had been rubbed and polished until it shone like gold. It reminded Edie of a miniature lighthouse with a little door to kindle the lamp and glass windows all around.

She was just turning the lantern over in her hands to admire it, when she saw a luggage label tied to the handle:

To Edie – Happy Birthday.
Much love, Uncle Peter.

"Oh!" Edie blushed. She felt her cheeks burning brighter than the polished copper. "Is it really for me?"

"If you'd like it," said Uncle Peter. "I thought it might make a change from a postal order. Something a bit more personal, now we've got to know each other properly at long last."

"It's beautiful," gasped Edie. "Thank you." She flung her arms around his neck. "I love it."

"I'm glad." Uncle Peter paused and looked down at his shoes for a moment. "You see . . . I thought it might be useful. I know you've been woken by my foolish fears in the night."

"No. . ." Edie blustered. "Not at all."

But Uncle Peter carried on, his good eye looking her straight in the face for a moment. "I've heard you bumping around downstairs."

"Only because I'm a clumsy oaf," said Edie. "I could trip over my own bare feet in an empty room, honest I could."

Uncle Peter smiled. "You are very kind. But I'm truly sorry about all the fuss and nonsense." He was looking at his shoes again and Edie wanted desperately to tell him there was nothing at all to be ashamed of, but she couldn't quite find the words.

"Trench terrors, I call them," he said. "Just old war demons coming back to haunt me in the dark."

"It must be horrible," said Edie. There was no point pretending any more that she had not heard his awful haunted cries.

"There are good days and bad days," said Uncle Peter. "It's just this beastly war – this new one – it brings it all back." A shadow fell over his face. Then he shook his head and picked up the lantern. "No more of that. Not today," he said brightly. "This is a lamp of hope."

"Yes," whispered Edie. "It is."

"You never know," said Uncle Peter with a smile, "it might just stop you falling down the stairs in the blackout, should anything happen to wake you up again."

"Perfect!" cried Edie.

"But it is only for using inside the house with the blackout curtains drawn. You mustn't light it and take it outside after dark," said Uncle Peter seriously. "Not even out here in the middle of the country. It's surprisingly bright when it's lit. It would only take one stray bomber like your Junkers from the other night. If they saw the light glowing, they might think there was a house below and drop a bomb."

"All right," said Edie. "I promise."

Then Greta came tearing into the stable yard.

"We're ready! We're ready," she cried. "Come now!"

Edie's birthday breakfast was well worth the wait. The eggs which Gus had been boiling had been painted bright colours as if it was Easter, and they had been laid in a nest of soft moss, decorated with petals and pretty speckled feathers from the hens.

"I collected all the feathers myself," said Greta proudly. "I asked the chickens first."

Edie laughed. "It's wonderful," she said.

There were flowers and sprigs of herbs spelling out her name across the table and little bunches of them in jam jars on every surface in the room.

Best of all, her chair had been made into a sort of a birthday throne, decorated with trailing ivy and white cow parsley flowers like lace.

"It's far too pretty to sit on," she cried. "I might ruin it!"

But they all insisted and, the moment she was

sitting down, Aunt Roberta appeared from the larder carrying a Victoria sponge cake with real cream and strawberry jam. Twelve candles twinkled like stars. Everyone burst into a rousing chorus of Happy Birthday.

"Go on, then. Blow out the candles," said Perky. "You have to make a wish."

Edie's very first thought was to wish for Fliss to visit. But, just as she was about to blow, she realized there was something far more important than that.

Keep Fliss safe, she silently begged the birthday gods. *Keep us all safe – Uncle Peter, Aunt Roberta, Gus, Greta and Perky – everybody that I love.*

But, as the candles flickered out, she worried she had been a little selfish. There was one flame left, so she gave another blow: *Keep everybody safe*, she added desperately. *And make this horrid war end quickly.*

"Three Chimbleys... I mean, three cheers for Edie," whooped Greta.

They all laughed and Perky banged a wooden spoon on the table. "Three Chimneys for Edie, hip-hip hooray!" he roared. And everybody clapped and cheered.

"Hip-hip..."

"Hooray!"

"Hip-hip. . ."

"Hooray!"

"Can I give you your present now?" asked Greta, rattling an old shoebox under her nose as Aunt Roberta cut the cake and poured Edie a glass of home-made elderflower cordial.

"Of course!" Edie beamed, wondering how she could have ever thought they would all forget her special day.

"It's a birthday crown," said Greta before Edie could even open the box. "I made it myself. Mr Churchill wanted to help, but the glue was too sticky."

"Thank you," said Edie. The cardboard crown was decorated with old sweet wrappers, yet more chicken feathers and even a string of Christmas tinsel. Greta had coloured the outside of the cardboard in with wax crayons and carefully written *HapY dirThbAy Ebie xxx* around the rim.

"I shall wear it for every birthday from now on, even if I live to be a-hundred-and-one years old," promised Edie, placing the crown on her head.

There was a little pile of gifts in front of her plate too. Wrapping paper was scarce with rationing on – even newspapers were allowed to print fewer pages than they used to – so there was no special birthday paper or fresh tissue but the gifts looked bright and cheerful all the same.

Aunt Roberta had given her a lovely copy of *Heidi* with pictures of snow-topped Swiss mountains on the cover. It was wrapped in old Christmas paper with holly berries on it and tied up with a bright red ribbon. All in all, it looked jolly festive.

"A very dear friend gave me that book when I was a little girl," said Aunt Roberta. "I'm glad to have someone to pass it on to now." Edie opened the cover and saw a faded inscription in blue ink:

To Bobbie,
The best nurse in all the world.
Love from Jim – Christmas 1905.

Edie was deeply touched. It was clear the book was very special. "Thank you."

She was about to ask who Jim was, but Aunt Roberta went on. "He and I always planned to go to Switzerland together and visit the mountains. Sadly, that never happened. Poor Jim died in the last war, like so many of the young men we used to know."

Uncle Peter stretched out and touched her arm.

Aunt Roberta smiled. "I was lucky enough to travel to Switzerland by myself when I was a little older. I took a train right across the country, all along the side of the lakes and deep under the Alps in long, dark tunnels..." Something about the faraway look in her eyes told Edie not to ask any more questions. She knew Aunt Roberta must be thinking of her childhood friend and how he never got to make the journey for himself.

"It's a beautiful book. I will treasure it," she whispered, thinking how much she'd love to travel through the mountains by train one day when she was older too.

"Now," said Aunt Roberta. "What else have you got? I can see plenty of other gifts..."

Gus hadn't wrapped his present, but it was a pretty little tin of colouring pencils, which looked quite smart enough all on their own.

Perky's present was extremely neatly wrapped in crisp brown parcel paper. He had tied it all up with a big string bow, which was very professional.

"I'm good at knots," he said, his ears going a little pink. "You have to be if you're going to work in the post office!"

Inside was a thick, green writing book with a

leather cover. "For your stories and whatnot," he blushed. It was much bigger and grander than the little notebook she'd had from him before. "There's only a few pages that have been ripped out of the front," Perky explained. "Aunty Patsy used to use it for her orders and that, until she got another one with squared paper which she reckons makes it easier to keep her sums in a line."

"Thank you," said Edie. She couldn't wait to fill the book with stories. "Thank you, everybody. These are the most perfect gifts I could ever have wished for . . . and the lantern too."

She felt an odd tingly feeling in the bridge of her nose and pricking in her eyelids.

"You're not going to cry, are you?" said Gus.

"No," she said quickly.

Uncle Peter chuckled. "You're just like brother and sister, the way you two bicker," he said. Then he handed Edie a bulging pink envelope with Fliss's curly writing across the front. "This came for you this morning too!"

"Ah-ha! I knew there was more than just that big, boring letter for you," she said, trying to sound cheerful. But as she felt the weight of the envelope, she knew what it really meant. If Fliss was sending something by post, it must mean she wouldn't be here to deliver it by hand herself. She wasn't coming. Not today. The prickling in Edie's eyes was back. She bit her lip. She wasn't going to let this spoil things – Fliss had asked her to promise to be brave and she would do her very best.

She tore open the envelope and pulled out a card with a picture of the Eiffel Tower and *Bon Anniversaire* written in fancy gold letters across the top.

Inside was one of Fliss's white handkerchiefs with a big red kiss in the corner – and, of course, a bar of Fry's chocolate, which had been squashed a little flat in the post. As Edie unfolded the hankie, the room was filled with the unmistakable scent of Chanel perfume. She held it to her nose and breathed in deeply as she read Fliss's message:

Wish, wish, wishing I could be with you today.
   I am sending this little memento until I can come myself and bring a really special gift.
   I miss you so much
   Love Fliss xoxo

There was no stopping the tears this time.
Gus didn't say anything and Perky didn't tease her

either. They both put their heads down and started to shovel in big mouthfuls of cake as if they didn't want to make eye contact at all.

"Cheer up, birthday girl!" said Aunt Roberta. Uncle Peter smiled kindly.

Greta threw her arms around Edie's waist, burying her head in her lap. "Don't cry," she begged. "You've got chocolate now and a crown!"

"I know," said Edie. She was half-laughing and crying all at the same time. "I'm not sad." She wiped her eyes with Fliss's hankie and smiled. She didn't want anyone to think she was ungrateful, not when they had gone to so much trouble and she had such lovely gifts. "I'm happy, that's all." And it was true. Even though she was miles away from home, and Fliss wasn't here, and the war had made her birthday a funny sort of thing where they had to "make do and mend" a bit, it really had been a wonderful day.

Chapter Seventeen

The Very Last Dark

Once Edie's birthday breakfast was cleared away, Aunt Roberta had to hurry off to the hospital and Perky had to dash back to the post office to help his aunty Patsy.

The children at Three Chimneys had chores too. Gus went to water the vegetable garden and Edie and Greta set off to see to the Twiglets. They were just fluffing up some fresh straw for their bedding when Mr Hodges' butcher's van rattled into view. The

Twiglets had grown fat and round already and, for a terrible moment, Edie thought the butcher might have come a few months early to take them away to their grisly fate.

"Glad to see you up an' about again, young lady," he chortled, as he climbed out of the driving seat. "Your aunt Roberta said that beef tea would do the trick."

"I'm feeling much better, thank you," said Edie, instinctively placing herself between the butcher and the Twiglets. But she breathed a sigh of relief as he opened the back of the van and she saw that he wasn't coming to take them away at all. He was delivering the churns full of food scraps from the pig club.

"Colonel Crowther couldn't run these up himself; he's had to go to London on business of some sort," Mr Hodges explained. "He'll be away for a couple of days. But don't you worry, I'll make sure these little piggies don't go hungry. After all, we want 'em to grow nice and plump in time for. . ."

"Yes. . . Well, if you'll excuse us," interrupted Edie briskly, "we must get on."

"Grr!" Greta was starting to growl like a Jack Russell terrier. She was not too young to know exactly what the butcher's job was – she had seen meat in his shop window in the village many times. Edie worried she might actually bite poor Mr Hodges on the leg if he mentioned sausages, bacon or, worst of all, a Christmas ham, in the same breath as her beloved Twiglets.

"We need to milk the goat," she said, grabbing Greta's hand and dragging her away across the meadow.

"Right ho!" called Mr Hodges, unloading the second churn and climbing back into his van.

"He is my number-one enemy," snarled Greta.

"Poor Mr Hodges. He is really a very nice man," said Edie. But Greta insisted on running back to sing soothing songs to the Twiglets the moment he was gone.

Edie was left to finish the rest of their chores alone.

As she came into the kitchen with the pail of goat's milk, Uncle Peter was opening the big brown envelope that Perky had delivered that morning. She guessed it must be more of his German translation work for the War Office. "Is it another shopping list from the man buying toothpaste in Berlin?" she asked.

"Hmm?" Uncle Peter was busy reading whatever was inside. "No, actually," he said, looking up. "This is something quite different. It might even be very good news."

"Really?" Edie was intrigued.

But Uncle Peter just smiled. "I better see to this. Maisie's still off with flu, I'm afraid. If you don't mind looking after Greta, shall we say lessons are cancelled yet again? You can tell the others it's in honour of your birthday."

"Brilliant!" said Edie as Uncle Peter hurried away. She knew Gus wouldn't mind a bit – it was clear now he'd only been pretending to get serious about school work earlier, so he could prepare her secret celebration.

"Help yourself to the rest of the boiled eggs for lunch. And there's some bread and another slice of cake for you all too. Make a picnic, if you like," Uncle Peter called over his shoulder.

"Good idea," said Edie. "Thank you."

She packed a little basket with an old checked tablecloth, the leftovers from the breakfast feast and the bar of chocolate from Fliss too. She thought it would be fun to take their lunch to HQ and eat it in the old dining car, as if they were going on a long train journey ... perhaps through the snowy Alps like Aunt Roberta had done.

Then she gathered all her other birthday presents around her and settled down to read the first few pages of *Heidi* while she waited for the other two to be finished outside.

By the time Gus and Greta came in, Edie was lost in the world of the Swiss mountains.

"One minute," she said, holding up her hand. "I just want to finish this chapter."

"Can I play with your new pencils?" asked Greta.

"Hmm," said Edie distractedly.

"And your lamp?"

"Careful, Greta," said Gus.

Edie glanced up.

"Can we light it?" Greta asked.

Edie sighed and put her book down. It was obvious she was going to have to leave Heidi and the Alps behind for now.

"We could light it," she said, opening the little door in the back of the lantern to show Greta how. "But there's not much point until this evening. We won't be able to see it glow properly until it's dark."

"And then we'll have to have the blackout curtains drawn," reminded Gus.

"Can't we draw the blackout curtains now?" whined Greta. "I want to have a go."

But Edie leapt to her feet. "I've thought of something even better than that," she said. "Come on!"

She found a box of matches above the stove, then grabbed the lantern in one hand and the picnic basket in the other.

"Where are we going?" asked Gus as they ran across the meadow.

"To the Alps!" said Edie. "*Heidi* gave me the idea. . ."

"Heidi?" said Gus.

"Well, *Heidi* and Aunt Roberta, actually," said Edie. "You'll see. Follow me!"

She led them across the top of the fields and only dropped down towards the railway when they reached the dim grey mouth of the tunnel.

"See!" she said triumphantly. "We can light the lantern in there. It'll be just like Aunt Roberta's train journey in the long, dark tunnels beneath the Alps. Even though it's the middle of the day out here, it will be black as night once we're underground."

"Golly!" said Greta, and she slipped her hand into Edie's. "The very last dark. . ."

"The very last dark," repeated Edie. "I like that."

But Gus shook his head. "We can't take Greta into the tunnel. It's not safe," he said. "What if a train comes?"

"There won't be any trains," said Edie. "Not today. That's why it's so brilliant. Perky and I saw the Italian POWs this morning. They're still working on the line. No trains can get through." Edie didn't like to admit it, but she would never have dared to come back here otherwise. She had been frightened out of her wits that first day when she and Gus had run away from the Snigsons' farm and hidden in the long, dark tunnel. She could still hear the roar of the train in her ears and see the lights coming towards her like a dragon's fiery eyes in the darkness. It would be different this time, they could walk right along the middle of the tracks without worrying if a train would come and they'd have the lantern with them to light their way.

"We could walk the whole length of the tunnel underground," said Gus. She could hear the excitement in his voice now. "If what you are saying is true, then today's our one and only chance. They're bound to have the tracks fixed soon."

"Exactly. Perky says they'll be done by tomorrow."
Edie crouched down in front of Greta. "Just so long
as you are not too scared to come in," she said kindly.

"I'm not scared one bit." The little girl shook her
head and squeezed Edie's fingers.

"We'll keep the lamp alight for the whole time and
I won't let go of your hand for a moment, I promise,"
said Edie. She put the picnic basket down on the
grassy bank and left it there so she could get a better
grip.

"That's good ... because Mr Churchill is a little
worried," said Greta, clutching him tightly.

"Then we will have to sing to him!" said Edie. And
she looked round at Gus one last time just to check
he was sure.

"Let's do it!" he nodded.

"You can take the lantern if you like," said Edie,
although she longed to have it herself. But Gus had
been a brick to agree to the expedition in the first
place and he was the oldest. "I'll be holding Greta's
hand anyway."

"All right," said Gus. "But you should light it and
take it for the first little bit. I'll look after Greta until
then and we can swap over when it gets really dark."

"Thank you!" said Edie. It was a lovely compromise. "Everybody ready?" Before Greta – or Mr Churchill – could get any more nervous, she lit the wick and walked into the mouth of the tunnel.

The glow of the old lantern was as warm and bright as Edie had hoped it would be. The orange light flickered and danced in the darkness. It was so much more exciting than a torch.

"It's as if it's full of fireflies," she called over her shoulder, and her voice echoed back. The tunnel was as dark and cold as she had remembered, but this time it was fun. She could hear the *plip-plop* of water dripping down from the roof.

She held the lantern up and saw her own shadow like a giant against the wall.

"I feel like a coal miner going down a pit," said Gus, his voice echoing too.

"A coal miner or one of the dwarfs from *Snow White*," agreed Edie. She had seen the Walt Disney film at least three times at the pictures with Fliss. "We could be mining for treasure."

"Dopey's my favourite," said Greta, but her voice was so quiet and scared there was hardly any echo at all.

"Here." Edie passed the lantern to Gus. It was

getting darker with every step they took and the pale light from the mouth of the tunnel was barely reaching them any more. "Shall we sing to Mr Churchill?" she asked, taking Greta's hand. Without waiting for an answer she burst into a rousing chorus of "Heigh-ho, Heigh-ho, It's Off To Work We Go".

All three children sang at the top of their voices, belting out the words and whistling or humming the bits they couldn't quite remember. It sounded as if there was a whole choir of them as the cheerful song echoed round and round in the tunnel.

"I reckon we're about halfway through by now," said Gus when they'd sung the tune at least three times and had a good blast of "It's A Long Way To Tipperary" too.

"Shh!" said Gus, although nobody had spoken. "What was that?" He held up the lantern.

Edie stopped and looked both ways. They must have turned a corner. There was no sign of light from either end of the tunnel.

She had heard the noise too – a tiny crunching sound as if something was moving on the stones which lined the tracks.

"It's nothing," she said, wishing Gus hadn't mentioned it. He would only frighten Greta. She was squeezing Edie's hand with an iron grip as it was.

"You're right. Probably just a rat," said Gus and Edie groaned.

"A rat?" Greta squealed and dug her nails into Edie's palm.

"Of course it's not a rat!" said Edie firmly, although her own heart was thundering now. "There would be nothing for the poor thing to eat. If it's anything it will be a mother fox with her cubs. She'll have made a lovely den down here and she'll go out every night to hunt."

"I like foxes," said Greta a little more bravely.

"Me too!" said Edie.

"Shh!" warned Gus again. He held up the lantern and put his finger to his lips. Lamplight arched across the curved bricks as he searched the tunnel. Just ahead, Edie could see the shadowy shape of a manhole. The inky-blackness of the recess was even darker than the rest of the walls.

Gus lowered the lantern a little. Light spilled down on to the rails.

"Ahh!" Edie screamed. She couldn't help herself. A leg – a human leg – was lying across the tracks.

Greta was screaming too. She was trying to pull Edie away. But Edie held her firm.

"It's all right," she whispered. "Shh! It's all right." At first, she had thought it was just a leg – all on its own – left there on the rails – as if it had been sliced off by a speeding express. But now Edie saw that the leg was moving. It was attached to a body. And whoever the body belonged to was alive. She could hear short rasping breaths, panting, as if the person was gasping for air.

Gus stretched out his arm and held the lantern forward so that light fell on the edge of the arched manhole in the wall.

"Hello," said Edie, boldly. There was no point in whispering any more. Whoever was lying there must have heard them long ago. Her heart was fluttering so hard she felt as if there was a pigeon in her chest. "Are you hurt?" She took a tiny step forward. Greta was still clinging to her hand.

Inside the manhole, there was the sound of shifting stones like shingle in the waves at a beach.

"*Bitte!*" said a thin, frail voice. "*Bitte tut mir nichts an!*"

"German!" hissed Gus.

Edie froze. Even before the lamplight hit the pale face hiding in the darkness she knew who it would be.

"The airman," she whispered. "*Our* airman." He

257

hadn't been captured after all.

"*Bitte!*" he said again.

Edie could see him clearly now as Gus held up the lamp. The young man was crouched and shivering, his dark eyes wide with fear.

"Come on," said Gus, grabbing Edie's arm. "We should get out of here." He tried to pull her away.

"Wait."

The airman held out his hand as if he was begging for something. "*Wasser!*"

"I am so sorry," said Edie slowly. "We do not speak German. We do not understand you."

But Greta's fingers slipped from hers and the little girl darted forward along the tracks.

"Come back!" cried Edie.

"Greta!" roared Gus.

Greta took no notice. She crouched down in front of the airman. "*Hallo! Wollen Sie Wasser?*" she burbled.

"What?" Edie was stunned. Greta was speaking German.

"Shut up," barked Gus. "Just shut up, Greta." He leapt forward as if to grab her, but Edie snatched at his sleeve.

"What's happening?" she asked. "I don't understand. Why is Greta speaking German? *How* is

258

she speaking German?" She sounded fluent to Edie.

"Oh, that's easy." Greta looked up, her face shining in the lamplight. "Our daddy is German, isn't he, Gus?"

"Shut up!" roared Gus. His furious voice echoed through the tunnel. "*Halt die Klappe, Greta!* I told you. Just shut up!"

"German?" Edie's head was spinning. "I don't understand."

Chapter Eighteen

The Fox

Edie took the lamp from Gus's trembling fingers.

She held it up so she could see his face in the dark.

"How can your father be German?" she asked. "You said he was in the RAF. You said he flew Spitfires for the British Airforce."

Gus kicked a stone against the wall.

"Well now you know," he said. "I lied."

"Is he a Nazi?"

"No." Gus looked her straight in the eye. "He hates

Hitler and everything he stands for. He's lived in this country for years. He's an engineer. He builds bridges. He worked for the British Government before the war."

"You don't even have a German surname," said Edie, still trying to make sense of it all. "You're called Smith. Or was that a lie too?"

"Smith – Schmidt. Same thing." Gus shrugged. "Papa changed it a few years ago. He sensed trouble was coming and it might be easier not to have such a German-sounding name. Gus is short for Gustaf and Greta is Gretchen. . ."

"The ration cards!" said Edie, remembering the first time she had met the children on the train. Gus had tried to rub away their names when Greta spilt the tea. He had thrown their evacuee luggage labels out of the window too. "You did all that on purpose, to disguise who you really were."

"It wasn't such a lie," said Gus. "Not really. Our mother was English. Our grandmother has pictures of the king in every room. . . We have lived in Britain our whole lives. We really are Gus and Greta Smith."

Edie glanced sideways. Greta was still crouched in the dark, babbling away to the airman. As weak as he must be, she had managed to make him laugh somehow.

"I didn't even know she remembered how to speak any German," whispered Gus. "We never use it with each other any more. As soon as Papa knew the war was coming, he made us speak English instead. He said it was safer. Even at home. Greta was so little then, I thought she must have forgotten it all by now."

As if to prove the point, she looked up at Gus and asked. "What's the German word for piglets?"

"I don't know," he growled. But Edie was sure he was lying.

"So where is your father now?" she asked. "If he's not a fighter pilot, I mean."

"Shh!" Gus put his finger to his lips and led Edie a couple of paces further away. "Greta thinks he really is in the airforce," he whispered. "Military police came at the crack of dawn and took him away as if he were a criminal. Now he's been interned in a prisoner-of-war camp. My grandmother thinks I don't know, but I do. It's what's happened to all the Germans who live in Britain. Austrians and Italians too. He's been locked up just because of where he was born – because he has the wrong passport. He loves this country but nobody even asked him who he would fight for if he had the choice."

"Oh, Gus, I'm so sorry." Edie was glad it was dark. She felt her cheeks redden. She couldn't look him in the eye. She thought of all the times she had complained about not being able to see Fliss. All the while, Gus and Greta's father had been in prison and Gus had been keeping it all bottled up inside him, pretending his father was away on top-secret missions. No wonder he had seemed so cross and sad sometimes. "You never got any post," she whispered. "I didn't even think to ask."

"I asked Papa not to write to us," said Gus miserably. "I didn't want everyone knowing where the letters were coming from. Imagine if Perky had seen a prison-camp postmark."

"He wouldn't have told anyone," said Edie. But she wasn't sure that was true – and the Snigsons would probably march up to Three Chimneys with their bayonets drawn if they ever found out the Smith children had enemy blood in them.

"Aunt Roberta would never have taken us in the first place if she had known we were German," said Gus.

"Of course she would!" Edie was certain about that. "Uncle Peter would have told her to."

"Not with his work for the government," hissed Gus. "Think of all those secret papers he has. They would have insisted we move on, or made him give up his job instead."

"Nonsense!" said Edie. "Nobody would seriously think that you and Greta could be spies . . ."

"Not until now, perhaps," said Gus and he looked back towards Greta and the young German.

Edie's stomach flipped over. He was right. They couldn't hide it much longer. Soon everyone would know she and Gus had helped an enemy airman escape from the crash. "Why didn't you say anything?" she gasped. "On that day when we saved the train." The airman had been shouting at them in German but Gus had shown no sign that he understood. Except. . . She remembered now. . . The airman had raced up the bank, waving a stick in the air. She'd thought Gus was going to fight with him, but instead he had joined him making flagpoles. "He told you what to do," she gasped.

"I wasn't the one who lied to Len Snigson!" barked Gus. "I wasn't the one who said we hadn't seen any enemy airman escape. You were the one who started that. . . All I did was back you up."

"Oh, Gus!" She knew it was true. She steadied

herself against the wall of the tunnel. Everyone would think it had been his idea to let the German airman get away. They would say Gus was a Nazi traitor. "What have I done?"

Gus shook his head. "What have *we* done. We're in this together. I am just as much to blame as you are, no matter what I just said."

"Thank you," she whispered. It was kind of him to be so noble – but it made no difference whose fault it was really. They were going to be in terrible trouble. All of them.

"What are we going to do now?" She groaned. "What are we going to do about *him*?" She pointed towards the airman slumped in the dark.

"You shouldn't point!" said Greta. "It's rude. His name is Karl. And he says he is very hungry."

Edie and Gus agreed – no matter what else needed to be done, they had to begin by fetching some food and water. The young airman must be half-starved by now. He had been hiding in the tunnel for days, surviving by licking moisture from the walls, as Gus discovered in a hasty German conversation.

"Yuck!" said Greta dramatically. "Mr Churchill thinks that sounds horrid."

"I left the picnic basket at the mouth of the tunnel," said Edie. "We could go and get that."

"Good idea," said Gus. "But we can't leave the airman. . ."

"*Karl*," corrected Greta. "His name is Karl."

"We can't leave *Karl* alone," sighed Gus. "Not until we decide the best thing to do. He might try and escape."

"Whoever goes for the food will have to take the lamp," said Edie. "And we can't leave Greta alone with him in the dark. . ."

"I'm not leaving either of you two girls with him." Gus dropped his voice. "He seems friendly enough, but you never know."

"And I shouldn't leave you here. Or just with Greta, either," said Edie. "If anyone caught you, they could say you were all making plans in German while I was gone. At least if I'm a witness, I could deny that."

"Then we'll have to take him along the tunnel with us," said Gus. "We'll all go together and when we're within sight of the entrance, someone can run and fetch the food."

"Right," said Edie. It seemed like a plan. Poor Karl was starving . . . and even she was beginning to feel she couldn't think straight until she had eaten some cake.

"I'll see if he's strong enough," said Gus. And he turned to Karl. "Can you walk at all. . . *Können Sie gehen?*" He switched reluctantly to German.

"Ja." The airman nodded and tried to struggle to his feet. He explained something to Gus, who translated that he was not badly injured, just tired and weak.

"Greta," said Edie. "You take the lantern."

"Me?" Greta squealed with delight.

"Hold it up as high as you can and walk slowly, just ahead of us," Edie instructed. Then she and Gus each took one of Karl's arms and wrapped it around their shoulders as they heaved him upright. He seemed to trust them. Or, at least, he didn't try to struggle or fight. Perhaps he was just too exhausted.

"*Heigh-ho, Heigh-ho, it's off to work we go*," belted out Greta, waving the lantern from side to side like a conductor's baton in front of them.

"Don't shake it too much or the light will go out," warned Edie.

"And keep the noise down!" hissed Gus.

"We have to be quiet now," Edie explained more gently. But after just a few paces, struggling over the sleepers and the shifting pebbles with Karl's weight, she wished they could sing. It might have helped to make the task seem easier.

All she could do was concentrate on putting one foot in front of the other without tripping over.

She was looking down at her feet and trudging on when she heard a familiar rattle on the rails. A chill ran down her spine. She knew that sound. It was the noise of a train... But it couldn't be. That was impossible. Perky had said the line was closed.

The rails rattled again. Louder this time.

"Quick!" There was no doubt now. She let go of Karl and sprang forward, grabbing Greta by the scruff of the neck. "Get flat against the side. There's a train coming."

Greta dropped the lantern and screamed, trying to scramble after it.

"Leave it!" Edie pulled her backwards.

Just in time, all four of them dived into the very same manhole Gus and Edie had sheltered in weeks before. They squeezed themselves together as an engine screeched past. It was only a small train, with a single carriage, but it was enough for Edie to feel the wind on her face and the soot in her throat. Her legs were shaking and the roar of the little train seemed to echo through the tunnel long after it was gone.

Karl growled and said something in German. Edie was sure it was a swear word. She couldn't blame him.

Greta was whimpering and clinging to her waist.

"You said the POWs were still working," said Gus, with a shaky voice. "You said the line was closed."

"They must have finished early," murmured Edie, but she didn't try to defend herself. It had been a stupid idea to come. Stupid and dangerous. . . They could have been killed. She felt as if she was going to burst into tears. It was pitch black again now and the lamp was probably smashed to pieces anyway. She lit a match with trembling fingers and held it up so they could see.

"*Hier.*" Karl stepped forward and picked up the lantern, which was lying on its side. Miraculously, it seemed unharmed. The train must have passed right over it. Edie lit the wick and blinked as the gentle orange glow of the light filled the quiet tunnel once again.

"This ist good!" said Karl in broken English.

"Yes!" said Edie. "Thank you." He seemed so kind and the light did make her feel a little better. Without another word they all stumbled on towards the end of the tunnel. Gus helped Karl by himself and Edie held tight to Greta and the lamp.

Greta held her beloved elephant, of course.

"Phew!" she said, when they saw the pale sunshine outside at last. "Mr Churchill did not like that one bit!"

As they reached the end of the tunnel, Edie blew out the lantern.

Karl tugged at Gus's sleeve and asked him something. Edie could hear pleading in his voice.

"He wants to go into the fresh air," Gus explained. "Out in the light."

"Of course he does," said Edie, thinking how terrible it must have been to be crouched in the dark for so long. "We could hide him behind that big tree there. Just while he eats his food." She pointed to a broad old oak. He would be hidden by the high bank on one side and the tree on the other. "Nobody could see him from the fields or from the train track either."

"All right," said Gus. "Just while we decide what to do next."

"We can always throw a picnic blanket over his head if anyone comes," laughed Edie, trying to sound more relaxed than she felt. She poked her nose out of the end of the tunnel and looked quickly in both directions. "Come on."

She darted out into the sunlight, picked up the basket of food they had left on the side of the bank, and scurried behind the tree.

The others followed. Karl winced and shielded his eyes from the sudden bright light.

"Here, drink this," she said, digging into the basket when he had sat down in the shade of the tree. She handed him the old ginger beer bottle filled with water that she had packed this morning. "I hope it hasn't gone too warm in the sun." But from the way Karl gulped the water down, it seemed it could have come fresh from the mountain streams of the Alps.

Then he ate all the boiled eggs and most of the cake too, cramming it into his mouth with shaking hands.

"I thought we were supposed to share," said Greta.

Edie's own tummy was rumbling but she shook her head. "It doesn't matter." She handed Greta a piece of bread. "Have this." She just hoped that cake and eggs weren't going to be too rich for Karl. Aunt Roberta hadn't allowed her anything like that when she was ill. He'd probably have been better with a little beef tea after having eaten nothing at all for so long.

"What are we going to do now?" she whispered, edging down the bank a little with Gus as Karl lay on his back and sighed contentedly. Greta was making daisy chains for him.

"We can't hide him any longer," said Gus. "We have to hand him over to the Home Guard. It's what we should have done in the first place. Colonel Crowther will do the right thing."

"But the colonel's not here," said Edie. She remembered what Mr Hodges had said when he delivered the scraps from the pig club this morning. "He's gone to London."

"That means the Snigsons will be in charge..." said Gus. He glanced over his shoulder, whispering even lower. "And you know what they'll do to Karl if we hand him over to them." He made a swift cutting motion with an imaginary knife at his throat.

Edie shuddered. "It's not just what they'll do to Karl; it's what they'll do to you," she hissed. "Imagine if they find out you're German and you let an enemy airman escape."

"Even Greta wouldn't be safe," said Gus. "Perhaps we should tell Aunt Roberta and Uncle Peter."

"No," said Edie firmly. She was surprised how strongly she felt certain that they shouldn't, although a big part of her had a suspicion it would be the sensible thing to do. "We shouldn't get them involved unless we absolutely have to. Not yet. People might think they were in on it somehow. They might say Uncle Peter was a spy too. He does speak German. . ." She couldn't bear the thought of anyone questioning him – shouting and raising their voices or trying to lock him away. He couldn't even be in the stable workshop without the door wide open. "At the very least he would lose his job with the government."

"You're right." Gus nodded. "We'll have to hide Karl. But where? He can't go back into the tunnel. Not now the trains are running."

Edie thought for a moment. "How about HQ?" she said. "It would be perfect." They could sneak Karl along the edge of the railway line and make him a bed hidden under one of the old tables in the dining car. Edie was sure it would be safe. Nobody except their little gang ever went there and it was certainly better than the tunnel. "It won't be for long. All we'll need to do then is keep him fed and watered until Colonel Crowther gets back," she added.

"It might just work," agreed Gus and he began to explain the plan in German to Karl.

"Tell him the colonel is an honourable man," prompted Edie as the young airman's face looked worried. "Say he'll treat Karl fairly under the proper code for prisoners of war, or whatever it is called."

Gus translated what she had said and Karl gave a solemn nod.

"Good," said Edie. "Then that's agreed." She was certain Karl was too weak and try to run away from the old railway carriage. He just wanted to be safe and cared-for now, waiting to go home again when the war was over.

"Come on then." She packed away the remains of the picnic. "Let's get going." She glanced anxiously along the tracks.

All they had to do was get the airman safely hidden in HQ before anyone saw them.

Chapter Nineteen

The Lie of the Land

"Ey up. Where've you been?"

Perky was waiting for them on the lane above Three Chimneys.

"Nowhere," said Edie and Gus together.

"Nowhere at all," said Greta, twisting her hair round her fingers. Edie could feel herself going red. The plan to hide Karl had gone smoothly, but they had agreed not to tell Perky anything about the airman unless they absolutely had to. Edie wasn't sure he would keep it secret if he found out. He might insist they do their patriotic duty and hand the prisoner over right away, even if that did mean leaving him at the mercy of the Snigson brothers. On the other hand, if Perky did decide to help, he would lose his job at the post office, for sure. Anyone accused of harbouring an enemy airman would never be allowed to deliver telegrams again. His aunty Patsy might even lose her position too. The only problem was going to be keeping Perky away from HQ for the next few days; they'd just have to think of something else to do if he suggested visiting the railway carriage. For now, he was looking at them very strangely with his head on one side.

"Funny. . ." he said, scratching his chin. "If you've been up to nowt, how come you all look so guilty?"

"Guilty?" Gus's ears were burning bright red. Greta was jiggling up and down as if she needed a wee. Edie gave her a hard stare. She wasn't sure the little girl was going to be able to keep their secret for more than two minutes. Gus had wanted to threaten Mr Churchill and the Twiglets with all sorts of terrible things if she said a word, but Edie hadn't been convinced that would do any good. Instead, she made Greta promise not to mention Karl by name or say the words "German airman" out loud. If she wanted to talk about him at all, she had to pretend she was discussing a fox. . .

"We just went on a picnic, that's all," said Edie, showing Perky the empty basket. "We felt a bit guilty because you were stuck at work."

"How the other half live, eh." Perky sighed but he seemed satisfied with their answer at last.

"We definitely didn't see a fox, did we, Mr Churchill?" Greta blurted out and then started giggling uncontrollably.

"What's this about a fox?" said Perky.

"Just ignore her," said Gus.

"The truth is," said Edie, thinking quickly, "we didn't want to tell you we'd gone on the picnic, because . . . well, because we were going to save you a slice of birthday cake and in the end we ate it all."

"You scoffed the lot!" Now Perky really was indignant. He chased them back across the meadow roaring like a wild bear. "You ate my cake!"

Greta squealed with laughter. "We didn't eat it," she whooped. "It was the fox!"

Gus and Edie exchanged glances as they ran. Perhaps Gus was right – it would have been safer just to threaten the Twiglets if Greta betrayed Karl, rather than dreaming up the whole charade of the fox.

"So," said Perky, when they had stopped running at last and were lying on their backs in the long grass at the bottom of the meadow. "Shall we go to HQ tomorrow morning? We haven't spied on those sneaky Snigsons for a while."

"Er... No," said Gus. "Not in the morning. I think I've got to do ... er ... Latin."

"How about this afternoon then?" asked Perky. "I'll ask Aunty Patsy if I can swap shifts."

"Erm... I might have history then," said Gus weakly.

"Really?" Perky looked amazed. "I thought you lucky beggars hardly ever did any lessons. Now it's starting to sound like real school."

"I'll tell you what," said Edie quickly. "I've got a much better idea than going to HQ. You know how you said there was an old signal box down the line in the other direction, Perky? Well, I'd love to see it."

"You would?" Perky raised an eyebrow. "I thought you said it sounded like a lot of dusty old levers and that the dining carriage was much a more exciting place to be."

"Did I?" Edie shrugged. "I don't remember." Although she knew perfectly well that is exactly what she had said. "I'm much more mature now. I've had a birthday, you know... Being so grown up, I've become interested in ... well, in signal boxes and things. I want to know how the railways work. It's all very well, waving to the Green Dragon and picking daisies on the bank, but it's the nuts and bolts and..."

"Levers?" prompted Gus.

"Exactly!" said Edie. "It's the nuts and bolts and levers, I should really know about." She wondered if she'd overdone it a bit.

But Perky nodded. "Fair dos. I'll meet you at the station tomorrow and we'll head on down to the signal box. Say two o'clock?"

"Two o'clock it is," said Edie.

That gave them the whole morning to see to Karl.

They woke next day to beautiful sunshine.

"Like spring has finally kicked off her shoes and wiggled her toes," as Uncle Peter said. It seemed he was having one of his good days, and the sun had lifted his spirits.

Aunt Roberta had already left for work. It didn't

take much to persuade Uncle Peter to let them skip lessons once more.

"Why not? Make the most of these sunny skies," he said. "Perhaps we should admit defeat and say it is officially the summer holidays anyway. September will be here soon enough, and you'll be at the mercy of those Maidbridge school teachers . . . a far stricter bunch than I will ever be."

"Thank you, Uncle Peter. You are a darling." Edie kissed his cheek, wishing she didn't feel quite so guilty about the bottle of his favourite pale ale she had sneaked out of the larder or the extra chunk of precious goat's cheese and the slice of ham hidden in the bottom of the picnic basket. She just hoped he wouldn't notice anything until tomorrow. By then, Colonel Crowther would be home and she could hand Karl over. She had decided it would be far better if she did that part alone. She was going to do everything she could to keep Gus and Greta out of it.

"I lay awake thinking all night," she explained to them both, as they hurried along the edge of the tracks towards the old dining carriage. "If I say I found Karl by myself, and I report that to Colonel Crowther, nobody will think too much of it. I'm just a girl who stumbled across a hidden airman. If either of you get involved, they might discover your father is German. They'll accuse you of hiding an enemy. They'll say you are spies – especially you, Gus, because you're older."

"I don't want to talk to Colonel Crowther anyway," said Greta. "He's scary."

"No he's not," scoffed Gus. "But Edie might be right." He looked over at her. "I just don't want you to get into trouble all by yourself."

"I won't get in to trouble," she said. "All I'm going to do is tell Karl to wait by the railway line tomorrow morning. I'll make sure it is around the same time Colonel Crowther will be driving up to Three Chimneys with the pig scraps. Then I'll dash out on to the lane, screaming and waving my arms and saying I've seen a German."

"It's not a bad plan. You'll probably end up being a hero all over again," said Gus.

"Oh, I hope not!" said Edie. "I'll slip away as soon as I see that Karl is safely in the care of Colonel Crowther. I don't want any more fuss."

There had been talk of them getting some sort of medal for saving the train. It made Edie feel guilty because she knew there'd be all sorts of talk about how marvellous and patriotic and British they had been and, of course, that wasn't true at all. The day they'd saved the train was the same day they'd first let Karl escape. It was also the day that he had saved her life, and the lives of all those people on the train.

"If anyone's a hero, it's Karl," she said out loud. "He could just have run away from that crash site and we would never even have known he was there. We owe it to him now to keep him safe."

"I agree," said Gus. They had reached the old dining car and Greta scampered across the log drawbridge to the door.

"Knock, knock! It is Snow White," she said, in the coded greeting the older two had reluctantly let her invent.

"And I am Doopey," came a sleepy voice, in a strong German accent, from inside.

"Not Doopey, Dopey, silly!" said Greta, flinging open the door.

It looked as if Karl had only just woken up. He stretched and raised his head, banging it on the table above him.

"Ow!" He let out a howl and the same German swear word he had used the day before. He blushed bright red and began to apologize. "*Es tut mir so leid...*"

282

"We have breakfast for you." Edie crouched down as he crawled out from under the table. She had brought along a tablecloth and a real china plate. She laid out the ham and cheese with a little bread. She had always known it would be fun to play house in the dining carriage. "And beer too," she said, producing a pint glass and waving the precious bottle of Uncle Peter's pale ale under his nose.

"*Wunderbar!*"

She had expected Karl to be rather stern and serious. She thought all Germans were a little serious. But he had big twinkly eyes and a wide toothy smile. If anything, he looked a little goofy – like the funny blond paperboy they'd had in London, who lost his job for posting a frog through snooty Mrs Hampton's letter box.

Edie smiled as he wolfed down the breakfast. Then Greta led him to the table and demanded that he draw her some pictures.

"Excuse me! Did I say you could borrow those, Greta?" Edie saw the little girl had brought along her new birthday pencils without even asking.

"Oops!" Greta just giggled. "Karl is going to draw me a fox," she explained. "And I don't have an orange crayon – only a sort-of-funny brown one which is too thick and a bit broken."

Edie raised her eyebrows. There was no point in arguing. She supposed this is what having a real little sister would be like and the thought made her smile.

Karl drew Greta a picture of a mother fox with four cubs all tumbling over each other at the edge of a wood.

"It's wonderful," said Edie. She could almost sense their whiskers twitching.

"He says the picture is like the forest where he lives," Gus explained, translating for Edie. "He has two brothers and a little sister called Brigitte. I think they are supposed to be the cubs."

"He must miss them a lot," said Edie. "Ask him how old they are."

But Gus was much more interested in quizzing Karl about the Junkers 88. He had brought along his book of aeroplanes and before long they both had their heads bent over it, chattering away in German.

Greta wanted to play a game where she and Edie had to be foxes. "You can be Mama Fox and I'm the baby," she said. "Pretend this railway carriage is our burrow. . ."

"All right!" Edie loved make-believe and imagining.

She knew lots of girls her age would say they were too old for such silly games, but she was delighted to have an excuse to play. "If only we had a nice plump duck for our dinner," she said, wrinkling her nose as if she had her very own set of splendid whiskers. She agreed with Greta, the railway carriage made a perfect foxes' den.

About half an hour later, Edie – or Mama Fox, as she was being – looked out of the window to check that there weren't any huntsmen riding by.

"Oh, no!" she gasped. A shock of horror ran through her. "It's the Snigsons." She caught a glimpse of the tall, thin figures of Donny and Len beyond the line of trees outside the carriage.

"Dear me," said Greta, in her Baby Fox voice. "I stole three chickens from their farm yesterday."

"No," said Edie, grabbing the little girl and pulling her to the floor. "I'm serious. It really is the Snigsons. Look!" She ducked under the windowsill and Gus came and crouched beside her. They lifted their heads a little and peered out.

The Snigsons were walking up and down the edge of the field, just a few yards away from the siding where the carriage was parked.

"What are they doing?" hissed Gus. The brothers seemed to be pacing about, just like they had done at the edge of the railway track before.

"Perhaps they're still looking for whatever it is they lost," said Edie, her heart thundering.

"*Sie messen etwas*," said Karl, peeping out of the other window beside them.

"What's he saying?" asked Edie.

"He thinks they are measuring," Gus explained hurriedly. "And he's right. Papa told me – it's what engineers do before they build a new road or a bridge or something. They have to pace it out to see the lie of the land."

"Why would the Snigsons want to build a bridge?" asked Edie.

"I don't know," said Gus. "But whatever they're up to, they're noting it all down." Len was scribbling something in a big book.

"How odd." Edie watched as he stuffed the notes into his big signalman's satchel, which was already bulging with other papers. "And what's that?" she whispered as Donny stooped to pick up what looked like a long leather cylinder from the ground.

"*Das ist eine Landkarte*," said Karl.

"A map," translated Gus.

"A treasure map?" asked Greta, her head bobbing up above the windowsill to see.

"Get down!" hissed Gus.

"Quick," said Edie. "Hide! They're coming this way."

Chapter Twenty

Maps and Plans

The Snigsons were definitely heading towards the old railway carriage.

Edie and Gus stared at one another in blind panic.

"What do you think they want?" said Gus, his eyes wide.

"I don't know." Edie shook her head. She could feel her heart pounding. "Hurry."

They only had a few moments to scramble into a hiding place.

She motioned to Karl to squeeze himself under a long bench below the window. He lay down with his fists clenched tightly by his side as Gus threw her the red-and-white tablecloth, and she stuffed it on top of the airman, trying to disguise him as best she could. Gus slid under the bench opposite as Edie grabbed Greta and crawled beneath a row of seats at the other end of the carriage.

Edie lay flat on her tummy, her nose almost touching Greta's, who was doing the same. She could feel the little girl's hot, frightened breath on her face. She put her finger to her lips and prayed Greta would stay quiet.

It was only now they were hiding that Edie realized she had made a terrible mistake. She had panicked. They shouldn't have hidden themselves at all. They should have concealed Karl and then stayed visible themselves, as if they were innocently playing in the carriage. That way, the Snigsons might just have poked their heads in or passed on by.

But it was too late to change their plan now.

The door flung open and Len Snigson strode in.

Edie could see his thick brown boots an inch or so from her nose.

"So," he said, pacing up and down. "Now we wait."

"Aye," agreed Donny. "We wait."

Edie tilted her head to try and see what they were doing. Len dropped the bulging satchel on the table opposite her. He started to unpack the papers inside.

"We've gold dust here," he said. "Get this into the right hands and we'll be rich."

"Aye," said Donny again. He had wedged the long leather tube between his knees and was gently easing out the rolled up document inside. Karl was right – it was a map. Edie caught a glimpse of little patchwork-square fields and the red lines which marked the roads.

Donny laid the map flat on the table and the two brothers stared at it in silence for a moment. Then Len punched the air.

"You can see the whole chuffin' railway marked out on here," he cheered. "Gold dust, that's what it is."

He was so excited, he punched the air again. Donny jumped out of the way. As he leapt backwards, he knocked a thick brown envelope off the edge of the table. The contents spilled on to the floor with a thud.

"Pick 'em up," growled Len, and Donny sank to his knees.

There were at least twenty or thirty photographs spread across the floor. He began crawling around, gathering up the pictures, just a few inches away from where Edie lay. Just one glance sideways and he would see her there, hiding under the bench. Edie had to bite her lip to stop herself from gasping out loud. She stared at Greta with wide eyes, willing her not to make a sound either.

If she'd stretched out her hand, Edie could have touched Donny's shoulder. One photograph had fallen halfway under the seat where she was lying. Her heart was pounding as she waited for him to turn and pick it up.

"Look here," said Len, jabbing the table as he pointed to something on the map. "You can see the railway bridge at the bottom of our field as clear as day."

"That's good, isn't it? Reckon that's just the sort of thing they'll need," said Donny, standing up.

Quick as a flash, Edie snatched the last photograph from the floor and clutched it to her chest before anyone could notice they had left it behind and bend down to pick it up. She couldn't bear to risk being seen all over again.

"Did you get 'em all?" said Len, as Donny stuffed

the rest of the pictures back into the big brown envelope.

"Aye," said Donny. "Reckon so." He glanced over his shoulder and nodded.

Edie breathed out slowly, her heart thumping.

"How long now?" said Len, pacing down to the other end of the carriage.

"Five minutes. Maybe ten," said Donny.

They both sank down on the bench by the window. Edie held her breath again. Karl was lying right beneath where the brothers sat, covered only by the thin checked tablecloth. If they looked down and lifted the corner of the fabric, they would discover him at once.

Edie felt a tug on her arm. Greta was mouthing something, her little face screwed up with urgency.

"I need a wee!"

Edie shook her head. She looked away, trying not to make eye-contact. Perhaps if she didn't look at her, Greta would stay quiet and hold on a little longer. But how much longer? Five or ten minutes, at least. That's what Donny had just said. But who were they waiting for? And why here, hidden away in the old dining carriage where nobody ever came?

Edie glanced down at the photograph in her hand.

It was of the railway – just a long straight stretch of track. Why would anyone want to take a picture of that? She turned it over and saw a line of numbers written in red ink across the back. It looked like some sort of code or coordinates from a map...

Her heart began to pound faster than ever. It was all starting to make sense. The Snigsons were spies! Why else would they be surveying the railway so carefully? They weren't engineers – yet they had all these photographs and they'd been out and about taking notes. Everything she had overheard the brothers say seemed to have something to do with the railway tracks. They were up to no good, for sure. But this wasn't just a few black-market sausages or an unlicensed pig: this was maps and photographs and documents.

Edie shivered as she remembered what Perky had said yesterday: *"Hitler would love to bring the railways to a standstill... Without trains the whole bloomin' country would grind to a halt."*

She'd laughed at him for sounding like an old man. But it didn't sound funny to her any more. It sounded terrible ... and true. The Snigsons had maps and photographs showing exactly where the railway lines ran. Britain's enemies would pay good money for documents like that. The brothers would get rich – and Hitler would get vital information. The German Luftwaffe would know exactly where to drop their bombs.

Edie wriggled her feet, trying desperately not to make a sound. She had been lying still so long she had pins and needles. But she knew what she had to do – even if it meant risking her own life, even if she might expose Karl's hiding place. She had to stop those documents falling into the wrong hands. The Snigsons were clearly waiting in the old carriage for some sort of secret meeting to hand over these maps and photographs. Edie had to get the papers away from here before that. She only had a few minutes left to act.

"Shh!" She put her finger to her lips to warn Greta to stay still and quiet one last time. Then she slipped out from under the seat and crawled towards the table. She snatched the map in one hand and the satchel in the other. Papers and photographs went flying everywhere as she staggered on to her shaky legs and bolted for the door.

"Oi!" Len Snigson leapt up from the bench.

"Stop!" roared Donny as she scrabbled to open the door.

"I know what you're doing . . . and I won't let you," cried Edie. She had no real plan – she just knew she had to get away and take as many of the papers with her as she could.

She scrambled outside and began to run.

"Got you!" She was only halfway across the log drawbridge when Donny Snigson's hand grabbed her collar.

"Like a rat in a trap!" sneered Len as his brother dangled her in mid-air by the scruff of the neck.

Papers and photographs fluttered down into the ditch below.

"What are you playing at?" Len was so close he almost spat in her face.

"I'm not afraid of you," roared Edie, even though her legs were shaking as they dragged her back inside the carriage. "I can stand up to you all by myself." She hoped Gus would understand and keep out of sight. But even if he got the message, Greta did not.

"Stop, you big bully! Put Edie down, right now," she yelled, scrambling out from her hiding place and hurtling towards Donny like a tiny charging bull.

"Well, well, well! So there's two of you, is there?" Len picked her up under one arm as she squealed and kicked. "Sit there, little'un, and shut up!" He plonked Greta down on the row of seats she had been hiding under. Donny pushed Edie down beside her.

"There's three of us actually," Gus crawled out from under the bench at the other end of the carriage.

Edie groaned. She should have known he'd never leave her and Greta to face the Snigsons by themselves. She just hoped that Karl would have the sense to stay hidden.

"Leave Edie and my sister alone," said Gus, drawing himself up to his full height and standing with his hands on his hips.

Unfortunately, he only came up to Len Snigson's chest.

"Ha! It's the little lad too," sneered Len.

Edie leapt to her feet, but Donny pushed her down again.

"You're spies!" she said, clutching the remaining papers and pictures as tightly as she could. "That's what you are!"

"Spies?" Donny gave a nervous laugh.

"What makes you think that?" Len's face gave nothing away.

"These," said Edie, waving a fistful of photographs. "And all those maps of the railway. I heard you. You said you were going to get rich. You're going to sell them to the enemy."

"I heard you too," said Gus. "That's why you been surveying the tracks. Not just today, but for weeks. We've been watching you, you know."

"Oh, I *do* know," said Len coolly. He took a cigarette from his pocket and rolled it between his fingers.

The corner of his mouth twitched.

"You're laughing at us!" cried Edie. "How dare you."

"Because you're going to look daft in a minute, lass, that's why. We're not spies," he said. "You've got it all wrong. You can ask Colonel Crowther if you like. We're taking all this information to him."

"Colonel Crowther's not even here," said Edie triumphantly. She wasn't falling for that trick. "He's gone to London, as I expect you very well know."

"Has he now?" said Len. He lit the cigarette and took a deep puff. "In that case, I'd like you to tell me summit." He pointed out of the window. "Who's that, up yonder?"

Edie gasped.

Colonel Crowther was striding along the bank towards them.

"Colonel!" She felt a great rush of relief. "Thank goodness you're here," she called, darting to the door. She thrust the pile of photographs and papers into his arms. "You need to look at these documents, Colonel. The Snigsons are spies; they've been putting together information about the railway to sell to the Germans. Look!"

Everything would be all right now. Colonel Crowther would take control – he would know what to do.

"Miss Edith, what an unexpected surprise." He smiled at her and, although he looked a little flustered, Edie felt better already. "And Master Smith and young Miss Smith too." He nodded to Gus and Greta. Then his eyes darted towards the fallen photographs in the ditch. "Pick those up," he said, clicking his fingers at Donny. "Now, what's all this about spies?" He stared over the top of Edie's head at Len.

"A load of nonsense, that's what. These kiddies have got the wrong end of the stick," said Len. Edie was amazed how calm he still seemed, even under the colonel's steely glare. She didn't feel half so relaxed. She kept glancing furtively towards the bench where Karl was hiding. She couldn't help it.

Gus was pacing up and down clutching his tummy, looking just as sick as she felt. They'd have to tell the colonel about the hidden airman soon enough. But, first things first, they had to deal with Len and Donny – it wouldn't be safe to reveal Karl until the two brothers were gone.

"You have to arrest the Snigsons, Colonel," she said. "Can you call for back-up from the Home Guard?"

Len laughed. "Tell them, Colonel," he said, as Donny dropped the muddy photographs on to the table with the map. "Tell them how it was you that wanted all this stuff."

"You wanted it, Colonel?" said Gus. "Whatever for?"

Colonel Crowther cleared his throat. Edie saw his eyes sweep across the map as if taking it all in.

"The colonel was helping us," said Len. "Not that it's any of your business."

"The railway tracks were built right across our land and we weren't never paid one penny for any of it," said Donny. "The colonel told us to measure the boundaries of our fields, then bring him maps and pictures of where the railway line runs and he'd help us with our claim."

"So you're not spies?" said Edie slowly. Their story seemed to make sense. She felt a hot blush creep up her cheeks. How had she got it so wrong?

"No!" Len snorted. "We are not spies."

"Honest, we're not," said Donny and he looked her straight in the eye. She half expected him to salute and swear on "scout's honour".

"Wait." Gus was standing over the map. He had laid the photographs out in a long line. "That doesn't make sense."

"Business matters never do make sense, especially when you're just a boy," said the colonel, striding over to the table. "I suggest you go back to playing trains. Leave us grown-ups to our dreary paperwork, eh?" He began to stuff the loose photographs into the satchel. "Roll this thing up, will you? Quick as you can." He tapped the map with impatient fingers as Donny fetched the long leather case.

"Wait," said Gus again. "It's all wrong." He held up one of the photographs so the Snigsons could see it too. "This picture is of the station." He picked up another. "And this shows the meadow below Three Chimneys... Why would Colonel Crowther ask you to take photographs of these places in a dispute about your land?"

"Exactly," said Edie, suddenly understanding Gus's point. "Those tracks are nowhere near your farm. They can't have anything to do with your claim."

"Er." Donny scratched his head.

"How do we know what these fancy lawyer-fellows need," said Len with a shrug. "We just collected what the colonel told us to."

"Quite so!" The colonel shifted his feet. Edie saw his eyes dart towards the satchel full of papers yet again. He kept glancing at them in exactly the same way she and Gus couldn't help stealing guilty looks towards the bench where Karl was hiding.

Why was the colonel behaving so strangely? He was jumpy as a rabbit. Gus was right. There was no reason for him to ask the two brothers to find maps and pictures of the entire railway line, just to prove something on one corner of their land.

"I think the Snigsons are telling the truth," she said quietly. "You're the one who wants all this information, Colonel. But it's not for the railway company, is it?" As soon as the words were out of her mouth she knew they were true.

"Now listen here," the colonel said, wiping his forehead with a red-and-white spotty handkerchief. "Time for you boys and girls to run along home."

Edie edged around the table towards the satchel full of precious papers. Colonel Crowther wanted those documents desperately – so desperately that fresh beads of sweat were already breaking out along his brow.

"It's you, Colonel," she breathed. "You are the spy."

Her hand shot out to grab the satchel.

But the colonel was quicker.

"Little devil," he cried, grabbing her wrist as he spun her round. His arm was across her throat in a headlock before Edie could even try and wriggle free. He was pressing down so hard on her windpipe, she couldn't even scream.

"Steady on!" gasped Len Snigson.

"Let her go!" roared Gus, tugging at the colonel's sleeve.

"*Hilfe!*" Greta opened her mouth and screamed. "*Hilf uns, Karl. Hilf uns, bitte!*"

"German?" Len spun round and stared at her.

"Why's she speaking Jerry-language?" gasped Donny.

Edie just had time to register the look of shock on everybody's faces, before the German airman jumped out from under the bench where he had been hiding.

Chapter Twenty-one

Capture

Karl had not taken more than two steps before the Snigsons leapt into action.

They grabbed one arm each and flung him back against the wall of the carriage.

"Don't!" screamed Greta. "Don't hurt him. He's our friend."

The colonel let go of Edie and sprang to the door. For an old man, he could move fast.

"Looks like I'm not the spy here after all. We

have some little German brats in our midst," he said, blocking the way out. Edie gasped as she saw that he had a pistol in his hand. He raised his arm, brandishing the gun at them as they slunk back against the walls of the carriage.

"Our father is German, yes," said Gus with a shaky voice. "But we are not spies."

"How do you explain our friend Fritz, then?" said the colonel. He waved the gun towards the airman.

"His name isn't Fritz," said Greta innocently. "It's Karl."

Donny snorted.

"Keep her quiet, can't you," said the colonel, his eyes flashing.

"Shh!" whispered Edie. "Come here." She grabbed Greta's hand before the colonel could turn the gun towards them and pulled her into a hug. "I can explain everything," she said, glancing between the Snigsons and the colonel. She needed everyone to stay calm. "It was my idea to hide Karl, not the others. It has nothing to do with their father being German."

"So why'd you hide him, then?" sneered Len.

"We were scared of you," said Edie, quietly. "We were afraid of what you would do to him before the colonel came back."

"And rightly so," said Len, twisting Karl's arm as the airman sank to the floor in pain. "Jerry scum."

"Don't!" cried Edie. "He saved my life. He helped us save the train too."

"A proper hero!" The colonel laughed.

"Yes!" said Edie, fury rising up inside her. "Karl is a hero. More than you. He stopped the train so no one would get hurt. He saved people's lives."

"English lives," said Len slowly.

"Yes." Edie nodded. "And Gus saved them too, even though his father is German. Think of how many people could have died if that train had crashed." She could see Len mulling this over. Even Donny was chewing his lip and nodding. She knew she had to talk fast and make the brothers understand who was the real enemy here.

"We trusted the colonel and so did you," she said. "He told you to collect all those maps and pictures of the railway. He made you act like spies."

"Enough!" The colonel was pointing the pistol right at her now, his back still blocking the door. "There'd be nothing easier than for me to shoot you all. I'd just say Jerry here ran amok. I'd say he grabbed my gun. . ."

"You tricked us," roared Len, realization flooding

his face. He clenched his fists, spluttering in disbelief. "You! The fancy colonel . . ."

He let go of Karl and leapt forward with a blood-curdling howl.

"Halt!" The colonel turned his gun on Len, stopping him in his tracks. "As you will know from your Home Guard training, this pistol is a Webley revolver, given to me in the last war. There are six bullets in it," he said. "That's one for each of you, I think you'll find. . . Two for you and your halfwit brother, three for the children, and I'll save the last one for Jerry. I'll say I bravely wrestled the gun back from him at the very end."

"I'll kill you with my bare hands," said Len. But he didn't move. His eyes were fixed on the gun trained on his heart.

Edie's own heart felt slow and heavy, not fluttering in her chest like when she had been frightened before. This was cold terror, not the heated panic of saving the train. Every second that ticked by seemed like an eternity as the six of them stood frozen, held prisoner by the colonel's gun. Only Greta was jiggling slightly, still desperate for the loo.

Edie glanced towards the window looking for an escape route and nearly gasped out loud as she saw Perky coming down the railway siding towards them. He was swinging his arms and looked as if he might be whistling.

Edie forced herself to tear her eyes away from the window. She couldn't let the colonel see Perky coming, but she knew she had to act fast. In less than a minute, he would open the door. That split second of surprise would be her only chance to set them all free.

She breathed deeply and made herself count slowly to ten. Then, at last, she heard the door handle rattle behind the colonel's back.

"Ey up!" Perky's cheerful voice rang out.

"Run!" hissed Edie, pushing Greta away towards the rear of the carriage. "Get under the bench and hide." In the same instant, she leapt forward, almost colliding with Gus as they both sprang towards the colonel at the same time.

"He's got a gun! Don't trust him," she shrieked, warning Perky who was still standing in the doorway, his mouth open wide with surprise.

"Freeze," ordered the colonel. Edie glanced over her shoulder and saw Greta still scuttling across the carriage towards her hiding place.

The colonel swung his gun around. There was a

flash of movement. Greta was still running as a shot rang out.

"No!" yelled Edie. But it wasn't Greta who fell. Karl leapt forward at the last moment, throwing himself into the line of fire, shielding Greta's body with his own.

Edie screamed as she saw him crumple to the ground.

Perky gasped.

The colonel raised his gun again.

"Coward," gulped Len. "You tried to shoot a little girl." Even he looked shocked as Greta crouched beside Karl's body, shaking him as if she was trying to wake him up.

Gus roared like a wild animal, charging towards the colonel. He grabbed the long leather tube which had held the map and swung it at the gun. The pistol flew from the colonel's fingers and spun across the floor.

"Get back!" yelled the colonel. He plunged his hand into his pocket. Perhaps he had another weapon hidden there, Edie thought wildly. She snatched the map from the table and threw it over his head like a sheet. It was only made of paper but it was enough to confuse him for a moment. He fought with flailing arms but she held tight around his middle. "Help me!" she screamed at Perky. "The colonel is a spy!"

In a second he was beside her. Without asking questions, he pulled a ball of thick brown parcel string from his pocket and began wrapping it round and round the map with the colonel trapped inside.

"Told you I was good at knots!" He grinned up at Edie as the colonel sank to his knees, trussed up like a post-office parcel. Len was beside them now too and he put his foot on the colonel's chest, pinning him to the ground.

Edie glanced over her shoulder and saw Gus gather Greta in his arms. She raced across the carriage to where Donny was leaning over Karl's body.

The young German blinked and smiled up at her. "Hello."

"You're alive," said Edie. "Thank goodness!" She sank down on her knees. But a patch of dark red blood was spreading across his shoulder.

"Run," she said, looking up at Donny. "Run for help. Please."

"Go," agreed Len. "You're the fastest runner." He stooped down and picked up the pistol from where it lay on the floor. He stood guard over the colonel, who was still parcelled-up in the map and squirming. "Bring the doctor and a policeman, if you can."

"Thank you!" said Edie, and Len nodded as Donny sprinted out the door. Then she turned to Perky. "Thank you too," she beamed. "I can't even bear to think what might have happened if you hadn't come along when you did."

Perky blushed. "I knew something was up," he said, looking at Gus and Edie and then towards Karl. "All that talk of signal boxes and whatnot. You were trying so hard to keep me away from here I thought I best come and have a look for myself."

"It's lucky you did," said Gus as Greta ran forward and flung her arms first around Perky and then around Edie.

For once she seemed lost for words. Edie stroked her hair. "It's all right," she whispered. "You're safe now."

"So," said Perky. "Is anyone going to tell me exactly what's going on. . .?"

When help came, the colonel was marched away under military guard.

"I hope you rot in prison," spat Len Snigson. "How could you betray your country like this?"

"There's nothing left to betray. Britain has gone to the dogs!" snarled the colonel. "It's full of scum like you and your halfwit brother. Hitler has the right idea. If only we had a strong government like the Nazis, then all the low life in this country would be flushed out. Britain could be great again. . . Truly great. . ." He was still ranting as he was bundled out of the door.

But Mr Hodges, who had turned up with the Home Guard, snorted loudly. "Nonsense, Colonel. You're only selling secrets because you owe money from betting on all those fancy card games you play in London. I reckon that's why you disappeared down there again this week, hoping you could win some of it back again."

Edie remembered the empty room she had seen when she peeped through the window at England's Corner on the day Greta got lost. Perhaps what Mr Hodges was saying was true and the colonel had gambled all his money away.

"Liar!" he roared as he was heaved into the back of the butcher's van, kicking and screaming, but still tied up tightly in Perky's knots.

Karl, meanwhile, was carried out on a stretcher and driven away to the same hospital where Aunt Roberta worked.

The children were desperate for news of their brave airman as soon as Aunt Roberta got home that night. "He's doing well and he'll make a good recovery," she said, after she had hugged each of them in turn and checked they were safe and well after their ordeal too.

"When Karl's strong enough, he'll be moved to a prisoner of war camp," Uncle Peter explained to them over dinner. "There'll be other captured German airmen there. He'll be well looked after and kept safe until the war is over."

"Just like our father, I suppose," sighed Gus.

It turned out the grown-ups had known the children were half-German all along. They'd found out all those weeks ago when Aunt Roberta went to Maidbridge to arrange having them to stay as evacuees. It seemed their English grandmother had never approved of her daughter marrying a German in the first place. She had been only too pleased to send Gus and Greta away.

"I saw the mess you'd made of your ration books and guessed you were trying to hide something," Aunt Roberta said gently.

"We knew you'd tell us if you wanted to," said

312

Uncle Peter. "But as to your father staying in a Prisoner-of-War camp, I've been doing a little digging. . ." He slipped his hand inside his jacket and pulled out one of his famous brown envelopes. "He is not our enemy. He has lived in this country for years and worked for the government, as you know. There were plenty of people who could vouch for his good name. Even the Home Secretary agrees he has no business being in prison."

"What are you saying?" said Gus slowly.

"I am saying," said Uncle Peter, "that if I were you, I might just go down to the station and meet the evening train."

"You mean. . ." Gus leapt up so fast, his chair toppled over.

"I am not saying anything." Uncle Peter smiled. But Aunt Roberta handed Greta a cardigan.

"Run along," she said.

Edie stood up too, but Uncle Peter put his hand gently on her arm.

"I think we'd better sit this one out, old girl," he whispered as the two Smith children tore out of the door. "We might not be wanted just now."

"Did you really get Mr Schmidt released?" she asked.

"Wait and see." Uncle Peter tapped the side of his nose. "But just remember, if he does come, it is *Smith*, not *Schmidt* – he changed his name."

Aunt Roberta smiled and Uncle Peter's good eye sparkled like a boy with a jar of secret sweets.

"Good job neither of you are spies, like Colonel Crowther," said Edie. "I don't think you'd do very well under interrogation."

"I have no idea what you are talking about," said Aunt Roberta innocently. "All I know is that I'd like a nice cup of tea."

"Right..." said Edie. But, when she peeped out of the door half an hour later, she saw Gus and Greta hurrying home across the meadow. They were leading a tall sandy-haired man by the hands.

"It's our papa. Our papa!" cried Greta.

"Pleased to meet you," said Friedrich Smith with a little bow.

"Pleased to meet you too," said Edie. And in that moment, she knew that everything would be different at Three Chimneys from now on.

Chapter Twenty-two

Beginnings and Ends

Edie was right.

After Friedrich Smith's arrival, things were never quite the same at Three Chimneys again. Greta and Gus were keen to spend time with their father, of course, and so the children no longer ran around together all day with nothing else to do but milk Mr Hitler or feed the Twiglets.

Aunt Roberta and Uncle Peter invited Friedrich

to stay for as long as he needed to. He and Uncle Peter sat up late into the night talking in a mixture of German and English and soon became the very best of friends.

Perky still called when he had time off from the post office and he really did take Edie and Gus to see the old signal box one afternoon. Greta said she'd rather stay home and build a chicken coop with her papa – she'd had quite enough of being a secret agent for a while.

"We've nobody to spy on now, anyway," said Edie as the older children all scrambled along the edge of the railway line. "The Snigsons are innocent."

"I wouldn't go so far as that," said Perky. "I'd bet my breakfast they're still smuggling black-market sausages and barrels of beer when they get the chance."

"Perhaps," agreed Edie. "But now I've seen what so-called respectable men like Colonel Crowther can do, I'm not sure it's really so terrible." She knew the Snigsons weren't good men, but they weren't bad either – not when it had really mattered.

"Len says we're welcome to come down to the station and watch the trains any time we like. He's even going to arrange for us to have a ride with the driver all the way to Stacklepoole if he can," said Gus.

"Can't say fairer than that." Perky nodded as if offering a ride on a train could cleanse even the most villainous soul.

"You boys would have tea with Hitler himself if you thought he'd let you drive an engine," laughed Edie.

Gus looked a little hurt, but Perky knew she was joking. "Only if there was cake as well," he said cheekily. Then he pointed along the line to the disused signal box. "Here she is."

The hut was small and cramped inside – and not nearly as good an HQ as the old dining car. But Edie had to admit it was fun to shift the dusty metal arms back and forward, pretending to control the fate of a hundred speeding trains.

"Here comes the *Flying Scotsman*," she bellowed, pulling on a disconnected lever and waving the imaginary locomotive through. "Send our love to the Highlands!"

It was like old times as they played for an hour or two and then headed back along the line.

"Did you hear about Colonel Crowther's house?" said Perky as they ambled home. "He had everyone fooled with his fancy car and neat garden, but he'd gambled so much money away at cards, there was barely a stick of furniture left inside. There was just an old army trunk stuffed full of secret leaflets supporting Hitler. There were pages and pages of the filthy stuff, all about driving out Jewish people and gypsies and only allowing folk who have white skin and were born in Britain to stay here."

Edie shuddered. Colonel Crowther had seemed so kind and gentle when they first met him – so honourable – when in fact he was rotten to the core. "Thank goodness he was stopped," she said. "After all, I think that's what we're fighting for, don't you?" It got lost sometimes in all the moaning about rationing and the hissing about hating their enemies but, in the end, this war had to be about defending a way of life that was decent and tolerant somehow. If not, what was the point in so many men and women risking their lives?

Her thoughts drifted at once to Fliss, as they had so often since Gus and Greta had got their papa back. She kicked an old fir cone along the edge of the track, hating the feeling that bubbled up inside her. She knew what it was. She was jealous. She hated herself for feeling that way, but she couldn't help it. She longed more than ever to see

Fliss, but there had been no word for weeks.

Perky headed back towards the village and, as they climbed over the fence into the meadow at Three Chimneys, Gus ran towards the big oak tree where his father was playing leapfrog with Greta.

"Join us!" called Friedrich, as the little family squealed with laughter.

"Sorry!" Edie waved and kept running towards the house. "I've got something to do," she called.

It was a fib, but she didn't want to be in the way.

As she bolted through the door, she found Uncle Peter and Aunt Roberta sitting in the kitchen. A man on the wireless was talking about the bombing of a German city by British planes. He might have been reporting a cricket match, he sounded so calm.

Edie couldn't bear it. There'd be children there, just like her and Greta or Gus and Perky... She remembered all the terrible things she had seen in London... The silver Cinderella shoe lying in the rubble of the Café de Paris.

"It's all such a waste! Such a stupid waste," she cried, and she ran upstairs and threw herself down on the bed.

She had only been there a moment, when she heard a quiet knock at the half-open door.

"Can I come in?" said Aunt Roberta, poking her head into the room.

"If you like," said Edie, but she stayed lying face down in her pillow.

Aunt Roberta gently touched her shoulder then perched opposite her on the edge of Greta's bed. Neither of them said anything for a while, they just stayed there listening to the sound of the other children outside with Friedrich.

Uncle Peter had joined them in the meadow and there seemed to be some sort of game of rounders or French cricket going on. Edie could hear the *twang* of an old tennis racket as it hit the ball.

"We could go down if you like?" said Aunt Roberta.

"Not yet." Edie shook her head. As she rolled over she was surprised to see Aunt Roberta had kicked off her shoes and was now lying stretched out on Greta's little white bed.

"This used to be my side of the room," she said, staring up at the ceiling above her. "I always liked to be in the bed next to the wall, because it made me feel safe and cosy. But Phyllis had the one you're in. She liked to be nearest the window, so she could see the sky."

"Really?" Edie sat up and hugged her knees. She liked the thought that Aunt Roberta and Fliss had shared this same little bedroom all those years ago. "Perhaps Fliss was dreaming of flying," she whispered. "Even then."

"Perhaps." Aunt Roberta laughed. "But mostly she was always complaining about how hungry she was and how cold ... and how many scabs she had on her knees from tripping up!"

"I wish you hadn't fallen out with each other," said Edie, blurting it out just like that. But she realized she'd been wanting to say it since the moment she had first arrived at Three Chimneys. "Was it really so terrible that Fliss had a baby... Even if she wasn't married? Was it really so bad that she wanted to keep me?"

"Oh, Edie! Is that what you think happened between us?" Aunt Roberta sat bolt upright. Her eyes were wet with tears. "It was never about anything like that. I never judged her for having a baby. Never!" The pain on her face told Edie that what she was saying was true.

"I was so happy the day you were born," said Aunt Roberta, swinging her legs off the bed and taking hold of Edie's hands. "You were so perfect. My little baby niece. A brand-new hope for all our family." She swallowed hard. "I knew I would never have a baby of my own, you see. . ."

"Because of Jim?" whispered Edie, remembering the young boy who had been killed in the war. The one who had written the inscription in the front of her book.

"Yes." Aunt Roberta's eyes darted towards the copy of *Heidi* on the bedside table.

"You were in love?" said Edie, and Aunt Roberta nodded.

"After I lost him, I knew I would never give my heart to anybody else," she said. "That's why Fliss and I fell out – not because I judged her, but because I knew how precious you were: the gift of life. Yet she was determined to go back to flying when you were only a few weeks old. I told her she had responsibilities. I said she ought to behave like a proper mother from now on. . . Fliss was furious. She never forgave me for trying to interfere with the way she lived her life."

"Oh," whispered Edie. "Was that all?" She reached out and took Aunt Roberta's hand. "You can make up now. I'm sure you can. None of that matters, not now."

"You're right," said Aunt Roberta.

Edie felt as if a great stone had been lifted from her chest – Aunt Roberta hadn't been judging her for who she was, or how she was born. She was just trying to look after the people she cared for. . . She was trying to keep them all safe from harm. That's what Aunt Roberta always did – what she'd done since the first moment Edie arrived at Three Chimneys. It was the same with Gus and Greta and Uncle Peter. And her patients too, of course. She was a nurse, just like the inscription Jim had written – a wonderful nurse, always looking out for everyone.

"There is one thing, though. I'm glad you didn't stop Fliss from flying," said Edie, glancing towards the window and staring up at the darkening sky. "That's part of who she is. She loves adventure. . ."

"I know that now." Aunt Roberta kissed the top of Edie's head. "I was wrong," she said quietly. "Fliss has always behaved like a perfect mother. She has loved you in the very best way she can. . . That's what being a mother is."

"Yes!" said Edie. "I suppose it is."

Then they both lay back on their beds again. Neither of them said anything else for a while. There was no need. They just stayed there, listening, as a train rattled past on the railway at the end of the meadow.

"I'll send your love to Fliss in the morning, if you like," whispered Edie. "I'll send it from both of us. Uncle Peter too. I'll send it by the 9.15."

"Thank you. I'd like that," said Aunt Roberta. Edie could tell by her voice that she was smiling.

The next morning, Edie very nearly overslept. The kitchen was empty when she came downstairs. The others must all have been out doing chores already. She didn't even stop for breakfast. She dashed out straight away so as not to miss the 9.15. There was no point in looking for Gus or Greta and asking them to come with her; they didn't need to send love to their papa any more – not now he was here.

She ran flat out across the long meadow and reached the fence just as the train roared past. She blew a kiss and waved and shouted. "Send our love, Green Dragon! Send it from me and Bobbie and Pete. Send our love to Fliss."

She leant against the wooden railings until she caught her breath again. After the huffing of the smoke and the rattle of the carriages was gone, everything seemed very quiet and still. It felt sad and lonely to be here without Gus and Greta.

Edie sat on the bank lost in her own thoughts for a while. So much had happened in the last week or so, and there were so many things she would have loved to tell Fliss if only she could see her. Then she gave herself a little shake.

"Come on, stiff upper lip!" she said out loud. There was no point in feeling sorry for herself. At least everything had been cleared up with Aunt Roberta. And things would return to normal soon, anyway. With Uncle Peter's help, Friedrich had convinced the British Government that he really was determined to join the fight against Nazi rule in Germany. He was going to return to London at the end of the month to help with the war effort and work as an engineer. Meanwhile, Gus and Greta would stay on at Three Chimneys for as long as they needed to.

Edie stood up and wandered back across the meadow. Mr Hitler was still waiting to be milked, and there were plenty of other chores to do too. . .

As she reached the big oak tree, she heard someone calling her name.

"Edie!" Perky was standing in the middle of the

meadow, jumping up and down. He seemed to be waving something in his hand.

She saw that the others were all outside as well – the adults were standing in a line by the door and Gus and Greta were pelting towards her.

"Look up!" cried Greta. "Look up!"

"What?" Edie shielded her eyes with her hands and squinted into the sun. What was Greta talking about?

"Look up!" bellowed Gus. "Can't you hear it?"

Edie pricked her ears. There was a low buzz far off.

"A plane?" she gasped.

"Of course a plane!" shouted Perky. "What else did you think it would be?"

Edie stared up at the cloudless blue sky and saw the shape of an aircraft coming straight towards her.

It was flying fast and low. Too low. . .

"Oh, no!" she cried. "Not another crash!" She couldn't bear that. The plane seemed to be so close to the ground.

"A Spitfire!" cried Gus.

"Whoa!" roared Perky.

They were right beside her now with Greta too. They all ducked down as the little plane screamed over their heads. Greta squealed and threw herself flat on the ground.

Edie put her hands to her ears. The plane roared away, circled over the train line and came back.

"Look! It's not going to crash after all!" she cried.

"Of course it isn't." Perky laughed and thrust something into her hand. "I delivered this not five minutes ago and your uncle Peter read it. . ."

Edie glanced down and saw that what he'd been brandishing in the air was a small brown envelope.

"A telegram!"

The Spitfire roared over their heads again. It was so close, she could see the pilot waving. She could make out the leather flying cap and goggles.

"Fliss!" Suddenly Edie understood. Excitement tingled inside her like electricity. This was the "beat-up" Fliss had promised for so long. She was here, flying low over Three Chimneys to say hello. She had come . . . in a Spitfire!

"Hello!" roared Edie. She didn't care about the noise of the plane any more; she had taken her hands off her ears and was leaping up and down, waving wildly.

The boys and Greta were jumping up and down beside her. She could hear Uncle Peter, Aunt Roberta and Friedrich clapping and cheering from the doorway of the cottage.

"Look!" cried Gus. "I think it's going to land."

Sure enough, the Spitfire had turned again over the railway line and was heading back to the edge of the flat meadow for a third time.

It was lower than ever. The boys cheered as the plane touched the ground and began to bounce along the grass.

"Phew!" Perky whistled through his teeth. "That's skill, that is! To land a plane like that without a runway."

Edie stood still and put her hands to her mouth. She couldn't quite believe what was happening. But, when the plane had come to a halt at last, she began to run. The pilot stepped out on to the wing, raised her goggles and lifted her helmet. Long auburn hair tumbled down her shoulders.

"Fliss!" There was no doubt who it was now. "It's really you. You're here at last," cried Edie, tears streaming down her face as she ran.

A moment later, she was in her mother's arms.

When they'd had tea and all the children had been allowed to sit in the cockpit of the plane, Fliss and Edie went for a walk alone.

They stood above the railway and waved as a little locomotive chugged by below.

"It was very brave the way you saved the train," said Fliss. She had her arm round Edie's shoulder, and Edie could smell the scent of Chanel mingling with the wild roses in the hedgerow along the side of the track.

"We won't get a medal or a fancy gold watch like you and Aunt Roberta and Uncle Peter," said Edie. "Not now everyone knows we tried to hide a German pilot."

"There are more ways to show bravery than with a medal," said Fliss. "You know you did the right thing and that's what matters. Here. Inside." She laid her hand on her heart, then slipped her fingers into the pocket of her flying suit and brought out a tiny package wrapped in soft pink tissue paper, tied with a silky white ribbon. "I brought your birthday present, by the way."

"Trust you to find fancy wrapping even when there's a war on!" Edie grinned as she pulled the ribbon off and turned the little parcel over in her hand. Inside the tissue paper was a delicate silver chain with a little charm on the end. As Edie held it in her palm, she saw it was a tiny steam engine, just like the Green Dragon.

"It's perfect," she whispered as Fliss fastened the chain around her neck.

"The trains have carried your love to me and now I am sending mine back," said Fliss, gently kissing the top of Edie's head. "From one railway child to another – Happy Birthday, darling."

"Thank you. I'll wear it always." Edie's eyes prickled and her nose tingled. But she took a deep breath. "I am not going to cry," she said in a croaky voice. "Not even after you have flown away tonight and I have waved to the last glimpse of you disappearing on the horizon. It has been a wonderful day and I am not going to spoil it with any more tears."

She held the tiny silver train between her fingers knowing no medal could ever mean more to her than her mother's gift and the love she would always feel when she wore it.

But, all too soon, it was time for Fliss to leave. They gathered together in the meadow to see her off.

"I'm sorry I can't stay the night. I've already taken a bit of a detour. They'll be wondering where this old girl has got to," said Fliss, patting the Spitfire as if it were a faithful horse. She pulled on her flying helmet. "I'll be back at the end of August for two whole weeks. I've booked in for a long leave and they can't change that."

"We'll look forward to it," said Uncle Peter, hugging Fliss tightly.

"Goodbye," said Gus and Perky. They both looked suddenly awkward, as if meeting a real-live Spitfire pilot – especially one who was a woman – had all been a bit too much excitement for one day.

"Take care, won't you?" said Aunt Roberta, stepping forward. "Just promise me that." The two sisters held each other for a moment, before Aunt Roberta broke away, quickly wiping her eyes on her sleeve.

"Come along, now. You'll want to get to the airbase before dark," she said briskly.

"Goodbye!" said Greta, clinging to Friedrich's hand. "I'm going to fly aeroplanes when I'm a grown-up lady too!"

"I bet you will!" said Uncle Peter and everybody laughed and cheered.

Edie dashed forward and flung her arms around Fliss one last time. "I'm so proud of you," she whispered. And in that moment, she knew that nothing else mattered. It didn't matter if she didn't know who her father was – or if people wanted to judge her for it. There was her and Fliss – just as there had always been. And, even if they were separated by miles of railway track or acres of endless sky, it was enough to know that her mother was out there, somewhere, waiting to return.

And the war had brought Edie a bigger family now too – Aunt Roberta and Uncle Peter, Gus and Greta, even Perky.

My railway family, she thought as Fliss climbed into the spitfire.

The propellers whirred into life and, with a final wave, Fliss was away. The plane bumped across the meadow and rose up, flying over the rooftops of Three Chimneys and off into the cloudless sky.

"Goodbye!" they all cried, clapping and cheering.

"Goodbye!" Edie ran to the edge of the meadow alone. She watched as the plane disappeared, growing smaller and smaller, until it was just a tiny dot on the horizon.

"Stay safe!" she whispered. "Please, stay safe."

Then the plane was gone.

As she turned towards the house, she saw that the grown-ups had already gone back inside. But Gus and Greta and Perky were standing a little way off, waiting for her.

Without another word, they all set off and started to walk in the direction of the railway.

"I'm so pleased we'll still be here together – for a while longer, at least," said Edie.

"Until the war is over," agreed Gus.

"We'll be like real sisters by then," cheered Greta, waving Mr Churchill in the air.

"We will!" agreed Edie. And she made a silent promise never to fall out with Greta like Fliss and Aunt Roberta had fallen out with each other for all those years.

Perky grinned. "You lot will have to go back to school in September, mind," he said. "Then you'll have to do some proper work."

"I know," Edie sighed. "But not yet. We've still got weeks of summer ahead of us." She glanced over her shoulder towards Three Chimneys and touched the little silver train hanging around her neck.

"Whatever happens, we'll always be the Railway Children," she said. "Nothing can ever change that."

Acknowledgements

Many thanks to my agent Claire Wilson at RCW and the whole team at Scholastic, especially my wonderful editors, Gen Herr and Sophie Cashell, and copy-editor Pete Matthews, for all your fantastic wisdom, hard work and support. I would also like to thank Keighley and Worth Valley Railway for answering so many of my questions over the phone and in person, either on the smoke-filled platforms or at your museums. But most especially, of course, I'd like to thank everyone at the railway for keeping those magnificent steam trains running, so that any of us can still hop aboard and imagine we might be "Railway Children" too!

Have you read
E. Nesbit's original
classic tale?

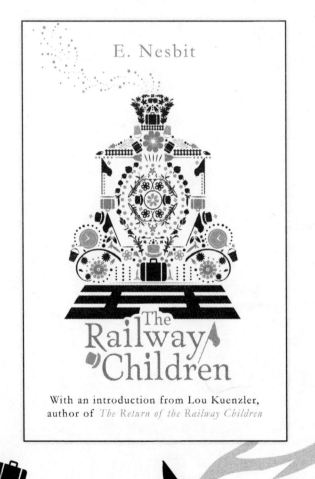

E. Nesbit

The
Railway
Children

With an introduction from Lou Kuenzler,
author of *The Return of the Railway Children*

Also available by
Lou Kuenzler:

FINDING
BLACK
BEAUTY

Lou Kuenzler

Anna Sewell

BLACK BEAUTY